P9-AGO-168

Pineapple Sugar

WITHDRAWN

C. PUNCH BROWN

Copyright page

No part of this book may be reproduced, digitally stored, or transmitted in any written, electronic, recording, or photo-copying form without written permission of the publisher. For information regarding permission, write to:

Darby and Allen Publishing Company,
P.O. BOX 449
HOUSTON, TX 77410

ISBN 978-0-9972774-0-1

Copyright © 2016 by Cynae Brown. All rights reserved.

Printed in Canada

Mommy,

There is not a day that goes by that I don't think of you.
I feel you in my heart. I see you in my children.
I hear you in my words.
Thank you for leaving a bit of your love behind so that I could
share it with those who need it most.

—Your daughter,
Cynae

I dedicate this book to my loving husband,
Joshua, and our little family.

Thank you for shining a bright light
on places in my life that were once dark.

chapter 1:

SAFIRI

When I was born, Mama gave me my name.

"People only listen to folks worth listening to," Mama always says."They'll listen to a *Safiri* quicker than a *Suzie* or a *Sally*."

Even if what Mama says is true, it's unfair, having a name most folks can't even pronounce. I don't think it's that difficult, but to the rest of the world, putting six letters together to say *Safiri* seems impossible.

I'm not sure what Mama's reason is for thinking that a kid like me could ever have something important to say. I'm no Martin Luther King, or anything. Trust me. *Safiri Day* will never be a national holiday, and no matter what, my name won't make one person actually want to hear what *I* have to say.

Besides the fact that I'm probably the only kid in the world whose problems start with her own name, I have never really been popular around the hallways of my school, Bringhurst Preparatory Academy. I can count my friends on one hand — three fingers, actually. Maisy, Kimberly, and Eileen. We've all been friends for so long now, that it's almost like they *have* to listen to me because that's just what friends do. To the rest of the seventh grade class though, something about me screams, "*Take your best shot!*"; like the time during art class when hot glue got dumped in my ponytail while my class made our Cinco de Mayo party ornaments. Then, there was that time during a class camping trip when someone thought it would be funny to hide three lizards inside of my sleeping bag. No one fessed up to either offence, and no one got in trouble. I, on the other hand, got the message loud and clear that Safiri Fields wasn't ever going to be a classroom favorite.

There are quite a few factors that keep me on the losing end of the popularity contest at Bringhurst Preparatory Academy. I've always told my parents that not having a cell phone is one of them. It seems like everyone has phones to call their own. Even Maisy, Kimberly and Eileen take pictures with the cameras on their phones while they're waiting to get picked up at the end of the day. It's almost like there's some sort of cell phone club at my school and naturally, only kids who have them can join.

There is absolutely no way of convincing neither Mama nor Daddy that I need a cell phone because they know exactly where I am pretty much every minute of every day. Even my "just in case of an emergency" argument got shut down by Mama.

"Baby, *I* am your just in case of an emergency. We go to the same place every day. If something comes up, Safiri, trust me. I'll know."

Even though popularity is not in my near future at Bringhurst Prep, my Mama seems to have that department covered. I'm not always enthusiastic about the fact that she works as a teacher at my school, but Mama has come to be the favorite teacher of almost every eighth grade kid who takes her English class each year.

In certain situations, having my mom work at the school I go to adds pressure to my life, especially now that I'm in seventh grade. I think it's more about the fact that I'll never just be an average school kid who gets in trouble *at school* and then gets punished for whatever she did *at home*. Instead, it seems like Mama has come up with some secret campus distress signal that's used anytime I do anything an adult sees as being lazy, disrespectful, or any other negative adjective — even if they have never taught me a day in their life. Once that signal goes up, in true Josephine Fields fashion, Mama peeks her head into whatever classroom I am in, and without a word, the teacher points to the door and my doom unfolds.

Doom, for me, usually begins with one of Mama's twenty-minute lectures on why whatever I've done "just doesn't make sense" — a phrase I've heard more than a few times in my life. The other part of it, though, is a task that only my Mama, the writing teacher, would create for me to do whenever I get in trouble: write about it.

Ever since my thumb and two fingers could hold a jumbo crayon, Mama, the writing teacher comes armed with a pencil, pen, and a piece of loose-leaf paper that she faithfully whips out of her purse no matter where we are. She forces me to report everything on paper — even when I don't feel like it.

I admit that I do love to write. I've always said that I want to be an author when I grow up. There is something about putting words together that makes the sun shine eight times brighter than it would have if I hadn't written them. Maybe one day, I will actually write a real book, but for right now, outside of the work Mama makes me do, writing is just my way of keeping myself out of trouble at school. My Mama, however, who is the president and lead member of my fan club, is convinced that I am going to be as famous as Oprah is.

I remember the day when Mama went out and bought a gigantic, dinosaur-sized yellow notebook for me so that I could write all of the stories I make up, in one place. I wasn't too excited when she shoved the spiral-bound notebook in my hands because yellow just so happens to be *Mama's* favorite color. Twelve years of having every shade of yellow glued to my life like the air I breathe has been more than enough time for me to realize that I've had my fill of the color all together. But every other spiral notebook that Mama has ever bought me for school has been one of the cheap ones that are only sold right before school starts in the Fall with the words "One Subject" plastered across the bottom. I don't know what excited me more: the idea that it was the most expensive notebook that Mama had ever bought for me in my entire life or the glittery, cursive "S" in the middle of its cover, which goes between standing for *Safiri* or *Super Girl* depending on who asks. Either way it goes, the yellow notebook is where I write my troubles away. It has become my way of fighting back without landing in the principal's office. Sure, I could just stand up for myself, but writing a story just seems so much simpler. My imagination gets lost between the lines of the pastel pages in what has now come to be known as "my book."

Those responsible for taking me down the path that leads to one of Mama's doomful lectures don't just bother me — they anger me. And for some reason, it seems like the angrier they make me, the more evil they wind up being in the stories I write in the notebook. Even though I could do without all of the kids that make my days look less like walking down the yellow brick road from Dorothy's Oz, and more like walking in a field of thorns, I have to admit that evil makes for a pretty good story — at least in *my* book. Maybe that's why a girl named Vivian Coats makes an appearance on more of its pages than I would actually like to admit.

Without a doubt, Vivian is just pure evil. Somehow, she knows exactly how to take me from blue skies and sunshine, to gray clouds and thunderstorms in less than sixty seconds. In reality, though, she is nothing more than a girl who thinks it's cool to make fun of anyone who isn't exactly like her. It's no wonder that Vivian is the star of one of the best stories I ever wrote in my yellow book. The words of it came together almost immediately after what I call "the Michele incident."

Michele was a new girl who came to Bringhurst Prep two Januarys ago. As soon as she walked in with her parents to register for her first day at school, the gossip started. Everything, down to the zebra-print charms on Michele's bracelets, made it clear to everyone that she meant business when it came to fashion. To Vivian, who had always been the center of attention with her name brand wardrobe, though, Michele meant trouble.

For someone like me, if Vivian isn't talking about my clothes, then she's comparing my thick, coarse hair to her long, smooth curls. It's pretty much the same for every other girl at school. For some reason, Vivian Coats always finds a way to make life miserable if you don't worship the ground she walks on. Michele though, seemed to walk to a different beat than Vivian did. She noticed things — good things about everyone.

"Cool notebook! Yellow is one of my favorite colors," Michele announced to me one day in the hallway. And those words were the only introduction I needed to know that we could be friends.

For about two weeks, it seemed like Michele was just what I needed. For the first time, Maisy, Kimberly, Eileen and I just kind of ignored Vivian. Michele was the type of person who automatically made you cool just by hanging with her. It seemed as if she didn't care about what anyone thought about her or us. Not even Vivian. Finally, I was part of a group that didn't get picked on between classes, and she no longer had to sit by herself at lunch. Michele brought something new to our group of three that had never been there. The moment that I let Vivian Coats get the best of me, however, was the very minute I lost Michele as a friend.

I hadn't even seen her coming. Since I didn't have to wait for a big group of people to walk with me to the cafeteria, I always made it to the line before everyone else, and met up with Maisy, Eileen, and Michele at our usual table, since they brought their lunches from home. On this particular day, Vivian got in the lunch line right behind me, and didn't say a word. I was focused on the hamburger and fries that were about to be dumped on my tray. Vivian was focused on making sure my friendship with Michele ended up in a dump. She had been ready to strike — just like a snake. Maybe if I had seen her, I wouldn't have even given a second thought to anything she said. I wouldn't have believed the lies she had been waiting to feed me.

"You know your new friend, Michele, is telling everybody that your mom buys your clothes from the *Goodwill* store?" Vivian blurted.

By this time, the lunch line had wrapped along the left wall of the cafeteria. Vivian and I were at the front of the line, where everyone could become our audience if they wanted to, and they did. Even the lunch lady, Ms. Wendy, looked up from the register long enough to see what was going on.

I gripped my tray and looked in Vivian's eyes. I didn't really know what I was looking for. Although I didn't like her, the unwelcome news still hurt, and it caught me by surprise. Vivian spoke while the others giggled behind her. Her face never changed, though. She seemed to be concerned – as if she was sharing the news of betrayal with me out of the goodness of her heart.

I've never been good at making decisions in front of crowds, especially not when I'm the center of attention. Even though I knew better, I fell right into Vivian's trap. Everything that I had learned about Michele left me. Somehow, I allowed myself to believe that since I had known Vivian longer than I had Michele, that somehow meant something. Even though I nearly hated Vivian, and she felt the same way about me, instead of keeping a good thing going with my new, fashionable friend, I messed up terribly and let Vivian erase all of the good things that Michele, Maisy, Eileen, Kimberly, and I had as a group.

Furious, embarrassed, and without saying a word to Vivian, I walked away, feeling betrayed. I felt the eyes of everyone in the cafeteria on my back. They were all watching me to see what I was going to do.

Talking behind my back is how she thanks me?

My mind raced as I marched toward the table where Michele, Maisy, Kimberly, and Eileen were sitting.

How could Michele do something like this? Was she ever really my friend?

By the time I got to my usual lunch seat, I had made up my mind.

"Michele, you need to go! I don't want to be friends with someone who talks about me behind my back!"

She had just taken a bite out of the ham and cheese sandwich from her purple and green lunch box, and had a mouthful so it took a few seconds before she could even say anything. Eileen, Maisy, and Kimberly just sat there, confused. I had been the one to make Michele a part of our group, and until that moment, had never been the type of girl to make a big production in front of everyone.

"What are you talking about, Safiri?" Michele looked up at me as if she didn't have a clue about what I was saying."I haven't said anything about you. I barely even know anyone here!" she pleaded.

Standing there, something inside of me started to question what Vivian had told me. My stomach tightened into a knot that made its way to the top of my throat. Suddenly, I felt like I was waking up from a bad dream. I scrambled, trying to figure out what was happening. My mouth was moving faster than my brain, though. By the time I realized I was walking right into some evil plan of Vivian's, I had already gone too far.

Everyone was still watching and waiting to see what I was going to do.

I looked right at Michele, wishing I hadn't started down the path I was on. Her eyes were filled with tears, but she didn't let them fall. She peered back at me, waiting for me to explain why I had chosen that day to try to embarrass her in front of everyone in the cafeteria.

"You know what? Fine!" Michele yelled before I had figured out how to make everything go back to the way it had been for the last two weeks. She stuffed her sandwich along with the chips, cookies, and juice that she had spread on the table, back into her lunch box, and walked out of the cafeteria door.

Standing there, watching my new friend storm down the hall, back to our classroom, I knew I had made a huge mistake. I looked over to where I had left Vivian and her crew standing. They were laughing and giving each other high fives as they walked toward me.

"Looks like you're back to three." The way Vivian threw her words at me made me so angry, I wanted to punch her. But I was too embarrassed to do anything but sit in my seat and put my head down.

The Bringhurst Preparatory Academy "Mama Signal" was automatically launched. By the time we got back to homeroom, Josephine Fields was waiting for me by the classroom door.

"So, you just believe what everyone tells you, now, right?" she questioned.

The look on Mama's face alone, told me she was disappointed in my actions. There was no way I could talk myself out of this one. There never was.

"No, ma'am," I whispered, barely able to hear my own voice.

"Did you think for one second that the folks who you chose to believe are not your friends and that they were making the story up?"

"But Mama!"

"Enough, Safiri!"

The lecture went on for about twenty minutes. When it was all over, not only did Mama make me apologize to Michele in front of my entire class, but I had to write a note to her parents, telling them how wrong I had been for listening to others instead of just asking Michele.

After that, Michele forgave me, but she never sat with us at lunch again. Other than an occasional "hello" in the hallway, she barely ever said much of anything to me.

The day I realized that Vivian had won a battle that nearly destroyed me was the day that I wrote the longest story I'd ever written on the pages of my yellow notebook. It was almost too perfect that the letter "V" already seemed evil and mysterious to me.

My stories weren't supposed to be real, though, and there was no way I was going to let Vivian's name be the first real name written in my notebook. In my world of words, I created a monster disguised as a little girl who finds any way she can to make my life miserable, as well as the lives of anyone who wasn't exactly like her. Naturally, the letter "V" was the first place I started when naming the evil villain in my story — a tale I ended up calling *Vanishing Vanessa.*

I had no plans to ever let anyone see it because it really wasn't that great of a story. It was just my way of getting over what had happened at school with Vivian. Even the story's title, *Vanishing Vanessa,* sounded silly to me. However, apparently, leaving my yellow notebook open on the kitchen table while doing my homework allowed Mama to see the story. Not even the big red circle with the 'X' drawn through it kept Mama from reading the title.

"Safiri, did you write this?" she asked as she gently yanked the notebook from my hands.

I was torn between feeling upset with her for reading my story, and feeling relieved that, after what I had done to Michele, Mama was interested in something good I had done.

To be on the safe side, I replied with a simple, "Yes, ma'am".

"*Vanishing Vanessa,*" she read again."Oh, my baby. I love the title! It's so brilliant!"

I was secretly praying that Mama didn't realize that the name of the main character in the story shared the same first letter as the person responsible for landing me in hot water in the first place.

Mama made me read the entire story out loud to her that day. When I had finished reading, she clapped her hands and told me not to forget about her when I became a rich and famous author one day.

It seems like even when Mama is upset with me, there is no way I can possibly question her love for me. She's hard on me at times, but my Mama is not only my inspiration for being caught up in magic and make-believe, but for the happy endings that many of my stories have. Ever since I was little, I have felt like Josephine Fields possesses some sort of magical powers that have always allowed her to see things that the average person can't even begin to understand. She has this weird way of knowing things even before you tell her. In my world, that's magic. To her, it's just living.

"You'll understand one day, Safiri, I promise," she says.

It's Mama's words, like these, that convince me that she is magical. Mama's promises are not promises at all. Instead, they are words that make you believe that she has taken a peek into your future.

My work didn't start out in the pretty, yellow, spiral notebook, and just because I have one now, it does not mean that every story I end up writing, lands there. I am pretty used to it now, but it still bothers me that *my* Mama hands me the trusty pen and paper from her purse without saying a word when something happens that would make the average twelve- year-old lock herself in a room and cry. Instead of giving me advice like my other friends' moms do, she makes me write *everything* down – even the stuff that hurts.

"Even the pineapple that turns out to be the sweetest in the grove is the sourest thing in the world before it's ripe," Mama preaches."So, the way I see it, there's no need to focus on the bad if you can find some good in there somewhere," she says.

Why Mama has to take something as simple as a pineapple and turn it into something I have to struggle to understand has always bothered me. But, Josephine Fields has always made it clear that she believes everything in life happens for a reason, and it's up to us to figure out the lesson in everything that happens, whether good or bad. Even as her daughter, I'm not allowed to argue with that.

"You never know what life lessons you may find hidden in your own words," she says.

I'm twelve years old now and have been writing for Mama my entire life. Either I'm not writing the right stories, or there are some lessons I just wasn't meant to learn.

chapter 2:

BITTERSWEET

My Daddy, Vance Fields, is a man of very few words. He and Mama are just about as opposite as they come. There's nothing anyone could ever do or say, though, to keep him from loving Mama. His face lights up with a smile whenever he talks about how hard he had to work to win her heart.

"Your Mama always had something to say about everything that had anything to do with me! She didn't know if she wanted to be sweet or sour with me," he says. "I would bring her flowers and she'd say she wanted chocolates. I'd take her to the movies and she'd complain about the popcorn. "That Josephine was about as sour toward me as a new, green pineapple straight out of the earth," he always tells with a grin. "It didn't take long, though, for her to realize I wasn't giving up, so she finally got sweet on me. That's why I started calling her Pineapple Sugar — she's sour and sweet all at the same time. A name like that couldn't fit your Mama any better if it tried!"

I think it is pretty safe to say that what Mama now calls pineapple sugar started with my Daddy. It's one thing to have a nickname but it's something totally different when you act like that is the name on your birth certificate. That is *exactly* what Mama does. At some point between all those years ago and now, she has made her nickname, Pineapple Sugar, take on a life of its own. For as long as I can remember, the yellow wallpaper in our kitchen has been covered in tiny little pineapples. The refrigerator is covered in pineapple magnets that hold up our family's pictures and calendars. The sugar jar that sits next to our stove looks more like it belongs in a Hawaiian pineapple grove than on the edge of our kitchen counter.

Just from looking at him, you wouldn't expect Daddy to have the rhythm and soul that he actually has, and you would never expect his singing to sound like a little slice of heaven. At least once every month, I can look for his tan guitar to hang around his waist from the green and white-checkered strap that seems to be as old as I am. Daddy goes into the garage, sits on the hood of his pickup truck, plays that old guitar, and sings his heart out, like he is standing on the stage of the Apollo Theater of Harlem. Usually, the songs he belts out are old radio hits from his high school days – songs that I've heard Daddy play softly on his record player time and time again when he thinks I've gone to bed. Every now and then, however, the newness of a melody that comes from the garage jumps up and grabs my attention.

Even though Vance Fields is a quiet man, his love for Mama takes him out of his soft shell. I was only in kindergarten when Daddy took to the cafeteria stage during lunch one afternoon at Bringhurst Prep, but I remember how everyone stood to their feet and clapped for him after he surprised Mama with a special song tribute to her for their anniversary. She was so surprised that she jumped up out of her seat, grabbed my hand, and ran onto the stage to give him a big hug and kiss right in front of everyone in the cafeteria.

The song Daddy sang that day was the song he wrote when he decided to ask Mama to marry him. It's a song that doesn't quite match the type of soul he plays his other music with because it's got "country roots," let Daddy tell it. He talks about that song at least three times each year, and every time, I still find myself grinning from ear to ear like I've never heard the story before.

Neither I, nor Daddy really likes the whining guitars and slow notes of country music. Of all the things Mama could have held onto from her childhood, though, it seems like the country tunes that her Mississippi-born grandmother sang to her during her summertime visits are the only things that stuck.

"Your Mama would always talk about how she and her *Dear Mama* — that's what she called her grandmother — would wash clothes, burn trash, and hang clothes on the clothesline all while singing as much Willie Nelson as they could," he remembers aloud. As much as she loved Willie Nelson when we met, I figured I had a fighting chance to get your Mama to marry me if I could play a little country song for her. So, I sat down with my old guitar, wrote one especially for her and called it *Josephine*," Daddy brags.

Josephine has always been one of my favorite songs. I've watched Daddy sing it everywhere – in grocery stores, at the park, and in department store parking lots. It doesn't matter where we are or how many times he has sung the song, every time Daddy sings *Josephine,* he closes his eyes and reaches for Mama's hand. It always sounds better to me when he plays the song on his guitar while he sings it, though. There's just something special about the combination of Daddy's voice singing along with the melody of his guitar. I think Mama feels the same way, too, because even though we all know every word of *Josephine* by heart, she only sings along with him if he's playing the music.

I can't blame her though. I can't help but find myself singing with the melody whenever Daddy plays it:

> *I'll take the bitter and I'll take the sweet.*
>
> *I'll find the beautiful day even if it's been raining all week.*
>
> *There'll still be time for a walk in the park when summer blossoms from spring,*
>
> *And I'll still find a way to hum when my voice ain't strong enough to sing.*
>
> *There's always a chance that life won't be perfect.*
>
> *So we've got to find a way to lighten up the load.*
>
> *So when the money's high and debt is low,*
>
> *When every seed that we plant grows,*
>
> *When they're no tears to cry and the sun always shines above,*
>
> *Just remember it's not always gonna be this way*

The bright side will sometimes fade away

But since pineapple sugar was my first love.

*As long as she's in my heart, trouble can't tear
me apart*

'Cause I'll see whatever life sees fit to teach

*Since pineapple sugar is always within my
reach.*

Even if he had never written a song and given it her
name, when it comes to my Mama, Josephine Marie
Fields, there is not one doubt in my mind that Daddy is the main reason she is filled with so much love.
Mama is the kind of person who has warmth and kind-
ness spilling out of her in everything she does. She is
always doing little things for people when they least
expect it — especially when it comes to our family. No
matter which uncle, cousin, or any other family member I ask about, Mama knows how to find them.

I discovered this family-tracking ability of Mama's
one day, while rummaging through her "junk drawer"
as I like to call it. Josephine Fields is probably one of
the neatest and most organized people I have ever met,
but you would never know it if you took a look inside
of her nightstand. I've been stuck by a sewing needle or
two over the years while playing in this never-ending

sea of my Mama's stuff. That was the case on the day I stumbled upon a little yellow, address book with small green pineapples all over it that was tucked underneath five old, fifty-cent coins. It held the smell of last Christmas's candy canes that had become so stuck to the back cover of the book, it was as if they actually belonged there. The first page had Mama's name, along with our address, written at the top of an otherwise empty page. As I began to turn the pages, it wasn't long before I realized what I was looking at: the e-mail addresses, phone numbers, and home addresses of everyone I had ever known to be a part of my big family. All of the names were handwritten, and arranged in alphabetical order. From Aunt Ellen, to Cousin Violet, down to Granddaddy Zeke, Mama had everyone covered in that old, pineapple address book.

At least once each year, I can count on hearing Mama preach about the importance of family.

"At the end of the day, Safiri, family is all you've got."

Looking at the pages of her pineapple-covered address book on that particular day, I quickly learned that Mama believed what she said.

I don't know exactly how true it is that your family is all you have, but a family like mine helps me write great stories. I can't even count the number of times that someone who looks like me has been the inspiration for the make-believe stories that I write in my book. When I was in fourth grade, instead of the regular Christmas cards that Mama sends to our family members, she copied a story that I wrote and mailed it out to everyone in the family. The story was called *Stockings and Stuff,* and was especially funny because the story's main character was my grandmother, who never could seem to buy enough pantyhose for herself.

"Girl, I got enough stockings to hang on everybody's fireplace at Christmas time," she would always joke.

My imagination went on from there. Gran became Santa's wife, who thought it would be a good idea to save money by filling up her pantyhose with the toys Santa was supposed to deliver. It seems like I got a million phone calls from my family that year. Everyone got a kick out of the story — especially the part where Gran's stockings ended up being the biggest and strongest toy sacks Santa had ever seen.

What we call *pineapple sugar* in our family is simply known by everyone else in the world as silver lining. To the Fields family, the idea of pineapple sugar is like a birthright that you are born to struggle with. It can either make your life better or anger you in the process of trying to find its meaning. When I think about it, somehow it seems like *everything* has a story that only Mama knows.

"Safiri," she always begins, "real pineapples and sugar are good partners, the same way that life's ups and downs go hand in hand. You've got to love it all together or else you'll spend your life only appreciating the things you think are sweet."

Not only has Mama made the phrase *pineapple sugar* a part of our everyday lives, but she has proven that pineapples and sugar taste great together, too. In fact, my favorite part of Mama's obsession is that I get to taste her cooking experiments that mix the two ingredients. She has made everything from pineapple candy, pineapple punch, and has even brought pineapples and sugar to dinner with a pineapple chicken and rice dish that she's cooked a time or two. Mama even tried making pineapple ice cream. Even though her first two tries on the ice cream were not too great, the third time was worth the wait.

What I especially love is that every year for Thanksgiving, Mama whips up her famous pineapple sugar cake. She only makes this dessert for our family's Thanksgiving dinner — no other time. The way that the pineapple glaze sits between the three layers of Italian cream cake makes the thick, sugary frosting seem like the perfect ending to the perfect story.

The pineapple sugar cake has definitely made me appreciate Mama a little more than I used to. Ever since I became old enough to draw pictures and write the letters of the alphabet, Mama has insisted on having me around while she cooks her pineapple sugar cake. The time that I have spent in the kitchen with her while she prepares it makes some of the best memories.

Each year, on the day before Thanksgiving, she gathers all of the cake ingredients on our small counter space. She mixes and mixes, stirs and stirs, until the smell of fresh pineapples fills our kitchen.

I'm not sure whether or not Mama rehearses lines for the lesson she gives while she bakes the pineapple sugar cake, or if somewhere, in between creaming the butter and sugar together over the years, she has just rehearsed a recipe of words that makes her lecture identical each time she gives it:

> *"You should never end a story without making sure you mention the lesson you learned from it."*

Pour the flour.

"It's your thank you note to life when you can find the good even when you feel like you are in a bad spot. Life happens and it's not always perfect."

Beat the eggs.

"There's no need to focus on the bad if you can find some good in there somewhere. You never know. One day, the way you end your story may be the reason someone begins theirs."

Mix it all together.

At last, Mama pours the homemade cake mix into the three, circular cake pans that she uses to make desserts with layers. When I was little, I would do a little dance around the kitchen for the cake's good luck right before mama closed the oven door. As I've gotten older, however, a quick wave has replaced the dance, even though I secretly move my feet under the kitchen table in hopes of a farewell to the scrumptious batter and hello to the delicious dessert. Mama never mentions it, but I'm pretty sure she notices my secret shuffle.

Once the oven door closes, the magic happens, as Mama says. But the magic she is talking about has very little to do with the pineapple sugar cake, and more to do with my life. Year after year, she turns the kitchen table into a writing workshop. Mama pulls out a sheet or two of white paper, and sits me down at the kitchen table.

"Safiri, what's your pineapple sugar story this year?" she asks.

Now, if you ask me, the question is pretty ridiculous. I'm twelve so, there is very little that happens in my life that Mama and Daddy don't know about. Not to mention the fact that somewhere, at the bottom of every purse Mama owns, I bet there is a gang of crumpled up papers with "pineapple sugar stories," as she calls them, that she forced me to write at some point. Still, year after year, I am forced to sit at the dinner table and write as Mama takes her time cleaning up the mess of pineapple sugar cake batter that is left on the kitchen counter. It's as if my Thanksgiving pineapple sugar story is the real deal, and all of the other stories I've written along the way were just practice; even more reason why all of the writing that Mama forces me to do is pretty dumb when I really think about it. I've never been short on persistence, however, not even when it comes to Mama's rules. But, by now, I have learned that writing pineapple sugar stories for Josephine Fields isn't up for negotiation.

"Mama, can I please go outside while you make the cake this time?" I ask.

"No, ma'am," Mama replies without a second thought.

My persistence hasn't paid off one bit with Mama over the years. I feel like I at least deserve a pat on the back for trying.

I have to say that even though Mama is a smart lady and knows a little bit of everything, I really think she made up this whole light at the end of the tunnel, feel good, pineapple sugar stuff. I've probably thought about Mama's pineapple sugar logic a million times. The way I see it, ever since she taught me to put letter sounds together, I have read plenty of books. Every story is different — just like the people in them. The happily ever after stories always end that way: happily ever after. You never need to search for the silver lining in the story because the good stuff is right there in front of you in black and white.

The sad stories are different, though. Those are the ones that challenge Mama's "pineapple sugar rule"... as I like to call it. You never hear about a crash, burn, and die story... where the author comes back and says, "Oh, but by the way, everyone was really happy because they learned something...even though everybody in the story jumped off a cliff." It just doesn't work that way — neither does real life.

The more pineapple sugar stories I write, the more I am convinced that life simply doesn't always give us pineapple sugar to work with. I just believe that sometimes, we get a bad batch of pineapples: the bitter and tart kind that makes your tongue burn if you eat too much. The sugar never comes. You just have to find a way to deal with the bitter, bad stuff.

Last year, I tried to help Mama see my point of view. It didn't work. I went as far as writing a two-page paper to prove the point that people can't always learn something good from a bad experience. I didn't really know where to start, so I got on my computer and Googled, "There is no such thing as silver lining in bad experiences." Like magic, a list of all sorts of professional folks who actually agree with the way I see things popped up. I found all sorts of people who had actually studied this type of thing in college — they had written articles, been on talk shows, and some even had written books. Since I was trying to prove a point to my matter-of-fact Mama, I knew I had better get some proof, if my goal was to prove her wrong. So, I printed everything out. I figured that even if I didn't understand everything that those folks had written about, Mama would finally see that pineapple sugar just wasn't real.

I cornered her one evening as she was making dinner. She was making lamb stew that night, one of Daddy's favorite meals in the wintertime. I caught her in mid-stew-stir as she stood over the stove, getting the meal just right.

"Mama, I need to talk to you about something," I started.

"Alright, baby girl, give it to me," she offered unsuspectingly.

Just as she had taught me to do, I started asking questions — questions that I already had the answers to, no less. My chest stuck out in pride as I made every point. The more I talked and the more papers I put down on the counter beside her, the more her jaw dropped. Her elbows tightened inwardly toward her body, and it seemed like her stirring got faster and faster. All of these movements, I thought, were signs that I had actually gotten through to her and made her realize that there was no such thing as pineapple sugar.

Just when I thought that I had won, however, I saw her left hand rise to rest on her hip — the same way she does when she is fussing at me for doing something I had no business doing. Every word that came out of her mouth after "you get your sarcasm from your father" pretty much sealed the deal enough for me to know that no matter what the so-called 'experts' say, Mama somehow has the upper hand on them. In other words, there never again was a question about the pineapple sugar rule in the Fields' household; whatever Mama says, goes.

To her credit, I can always rest assured that each year, Mama will have the yellow basket filled with crayons, markers, colored pencils, and pens, on the right hand side of the dinner table — the spot where I eat my dinner each night. I never have to do anything but bring my thoughts of being thankful to the table, and write.

When I was little, there would always be more pictures than words on my page by the time Mama took the pineapple sugar cake from the oven. Now, I just write, until my hand hurts. I admit that I haven't gotten too old, though to taste the remains of sweet cake batter left in the mixing bowl right before she washes it out in the sink.

From the time Mama puts the pineapple sugar cake into the oven until the time she sticks the first toothpick in to see if it's done, I always seem to fit three-hundred, sixty-five days worth of my untold story onto a few pages of loose-leaf paper. Mama is an unfair judge, though. It seems like no matter how much I write from the time I sit down to the time she takes the pineapple sugar cake out of the oven, she always wants me to do more. Mama makes sure that I not only write about things we have celebrated over the year, like good grades on my report card, but that I also don't leave out the bad experiences. By the time the cake cools, both my hand and brain hurt from all the lessons I've had to write about. I've gotten pretty good at writing about the good experiences. The bad ones, though still seem to be the trickiest.

chapter 3:
THE JOURNEY BEGINS

I t never fails. Every time my math teacher, Ms. Darcy, is out sick, we get a substitute teacher who insists on calling roll.

"Jennifer?" The teacher calls roll from the class roster.

"Here!"

"Erin?"

"Present!"

"Sa...Sifi...Safffire?"

"It's Safiri, and I'm here," I reply slyly.

Attendance time for someone with a name like mine is kind of like an awful song on repeat that you can't stop. Eventually, you join in and start singing along. It always amazes me how substitute teachers usually have no clue how to pronounce my name. In first grade, when the teacher called me *Saffir*, it embarrassed me. In second grade, it hurt a little when Mrs. Clifford reminded me of how different my name is by simplifying it to *Sofia* when she took attendance. But, by third grade, both my eye roll and shrugged response to the laughs that came after the teacher called me *Safifi*, had been perfected.

Ever since then, *"It's Safiri, and I'm here"* is the slick remark that has rolled off my tongue without a second thought.

There must be something in the April air that's making people sick because Mama called in sick today, too. I don't know, though. Mrs. Darcy sneezed about thirty-one times in a row during library time yesterday — enough times for every, single person in the class to say, "Bless you," at least once. Mama is different, though. Last Thursday when I went to see her during lunch, I found her at her desk with her head buried in the palms of her hands. I stood in the doorway watching and waiting for her to notice me, but she didn't. She pulled her hair, which drifted to the middle of her back, over her shoulders. As she slid her fingertips down to the roots of her locked hair, her eyes remained closed.

"Mama?"

She jumped at the sound of my voice. From the look she gave me, I could tell she knew I was worried about her.

"I'm just resting, baby," she assured me calmly.

As far as I know, Mama has never lied — at least not to me. Daddy will do his best to keep things from me, especially if it's bad news. Mama, on the other hand is pretty straightforward. With all of her pineapple sugar talk, she can find a way to talk about just anything.

"You always need to know the whole truth," she always preaches. "As long as you ask a good question in this house, Safiri, the least I can do is always give you an honest answer, no matter what."

That's why this time seems different. I've known my Mama long enough to know what it looks like when she's not being her usual self. It comes down to a single root of her dreadlocked hair — she twists it. Whenever Josephine Fields extends the tips of her right hand all the way back to the bottom left-hand side of her neckline and starts to twist her wrist, I can guarantee that there is something that's not right in the world.

Sunday breakfast in the Fields' house starts at 7:00 a.m. Every Sunday morning, Mama and Daddy wake up early and make biscuits, eggs, grits, and most importantly, bacon. Everything else is great, but it's usually the smell of bacon that travels all the way from the kitchen to my room to make sure that I'm fully awake. Daddy always tries to be funny and yells, *"Cock-a-doodle-do!"* to let me know when it's time to come eat, but by then, bacon has already done that job.

I love Sunday breakfast because, as a family, we make time to talk about whatever is on our minds — from where we want our next family vacation to be, to what we want Mama to cook for dinner. Between Mama, Daddy, and me, there is never a shortage of things to say, and Sunday breakfast is the only time that we have to just sit and talk without having to rush off to grade papers, do homework, or work on things that need to be done around the house.

This morning, there is no smell of bacon greeting me. I lie in bed and look at the clock.

7:13 a.m. I don't hear the usual clanging of pots and pans that usually happens when Daddy joins Mama in the kitchen to cook.

Did I miss Daddy's call to breakfast?

"Cock-a-doodle-do!"

The latest Daddy has ever called me down for Sunday morning breakfast is 7:02 a.m. and that was only because it was daylight savings time and Mama forgot to change the kitchen clock the night before.

As I slide my robe over my shoulders, and slide on my house shoes, I can't help but notice the day already feels different.

"Good morning, Daddy. Good morning...."

My voice trails off into the pineapple-covered walls of our yellow kitchen. I look around for Mama, but she's missing.

"Uh...your Mama's just tired, Safiri. Don't worry."

Daddy's an awful liar. I know better than to believe that after nearly twelve years of the same Sunday routine, Mama is missing breakfast because she's a little sleepy. I hate it when my parents act like I'm still a clueless baby. It's just about as bad as an adult spelling a swear word in front of a kid who just won a spelling bee. I'm Josephine's daughter, which means I know more than folks usually give me credit for.

"So what happened at school this week, baby girl?" Daddy asked with an awkward smile.

Having Sunday morning conversation at the table without Mama doesn't even feel right.

"Daddy, is Mama going to be alright?

Daddy keeps chewing as he looks down into the bowl of cereal we are calling breakfast this morning.

Somewhere inside of his Frosted Flakes, I think he is looking for what to say to me.

"Yes! I'm going to be fine, baby!"

Mama waltzes in like nothing's any different from other Sunday mornings. She reaches for the cereal box, and fills her bowl to the brim before pouring in just enough milk to make the frosted flakes damp.

"Mama?"

Daddy quickly glances at Mama, but then immediately returns his gaze back down to the soggy cereal in his bowl.

"What's going on, sweetie?" She responds in a high, pitched tone.

I wasn't able to put the words together that would get to the bottom of why Mama had been late to breakfast for the first time in forever. The way I began to babble– throwing "uh" and "ums" around as if they meant something, it seemed like Michael Jackson — not Mama, had sat down at the breakfast table with me.

"Where's the bacon?" I blurt out.

How or why these are the only words that find their way out of my mouth, I have no idea. I miss my chance to find out what's going on with Mama, but still, all I can do is laugh along with my parents.

We all laugh until we barely have any air left to breathe. By the time we recover, it's time to clear the table and get dressed.

"Alright, you two. Safiri, go get dressed, baby."

I take my bowl to the sink and pour the leftover milk down the drain. I turn to ask Mama if she's OK.

"Mama?"

But she's already left the kitchen.

We've been members of Trinity Zion Baptist Church my entire life. I was seven when we got a new sign outside with the pastor's name on it.

"That settles it. I'm staying," Rev. Bingham had joked. He has been the pastor of our church since Mama was seventeen-years-old, but when the last big hurricane knocked down the sign on the church's front lawn four years ago, nobody bothered to get it fixed — not even Rev. Bingham.

Mama grew up in Trinity Zion. She and Daddy got married here. So, when Mama told Daddy that we were going to fix the broken sign, there really wasn't much he had to say about it.

"Seems like somebody should fix that sign, Vance."

"Yep."

"We're gonna fix that sign, Vance."

"Yep."

There was a picnic on the front lawn of the church the day it went up. Mama, Daddy, and I stood next to Reverend Bingham as the cameras flashed. It seemed like I held smiles until my cheeks got numb.

We don't go to service *every* Sunday, but we go enough. Today, though, you would think that Mama's got keys to this place the way she's making her way to the front of the sanctuary. Usually, we sit near the back, right hand corner of the church, so that when it all ends, we can make a break for the door without all the traffic. Not today, though.

Mama stands through every song the choir sings. She lifts her hands and moves side to side with the rhythm of every song. As the choir sings its last song, Mama seems to break. The tears in her eyes can no longer rest. As they fall, Mama cries softly. She tries to wipe her face, but her hands cannot keep up.

Daddy stands to put his hands gently around Mama's shoulder. She seems to buckle under his touch as she gives in to her sobbing.

> *When my way grows drear,*
> *Precious Lord linger near.*
> *When my life is almost gone...*

The choir's song seems to cut straight to Mama's heart. There's nothing I can do as the church ushers gather around Mama and Daddy. As their church fans seem to calm Mama down, they don't do much for her tears.

Hear my cry, hear my call
Hold my hand, lest I fall...
Precious Lord, take my hand
Lead me home.

I watch Reverend Bingham come slowly out of the pulpit to stand in front of the church. As the choir's song comes to an end, he extends his hand toward Mama and Daddy.

Well, this is new.

My parents walk toward Reverend Bingham's outstretched hand — Daddy still holding Mama close.

"Church, it's prayer time for this family."

Reverend Bingham's left hand grips the microphone tightly as he moves his right hand from the top of Mama's head to Daddy's.

Members of the congregation close their eyes, bow their heads, and stretch their arms toward Mama and Daddy. As the organist plays the melody of the choir's last selection, Mama's tears stop. Mama turns and looks at me. Her eyes are red from crying. She holds her hand out for me to come, but I've always been told not to move while the preacher is praying. I shake my head from side to side to let Mama know I don't want to come.

"*Okay, baby,*" Mama mouths silently.

She turns back toward Reverend Bingham just in time to close her eyes before he says, "Amen."

Something just isn't right. As a family, we never have secrets or keep things from one another, but now, both Mama and Daddy are keeping something from me — I'm sure of it. But not for long. I'm determined to figure out exactly what it is.

I watch Mama and Daddy come back to the pew where we are sitting. The organist continues the melody while lifting his hand to direct the choir as Reverend Bingham makes his way back up to the pulpit

Precious Lord, take my hand
Lead me home.

Mama has been missing more days of school than she ever has. For a teacher like Mama, who lives and breathes everything about school and teaching children, missing any days — even when she's sick, is a bad sign.

Her students have started to ask me questions about Mama, questions I don't really have the answers to. Even though I never have any real news about when Mama plans on coming back to work, they always give me their "Feel better, Mrs. Fields" notes to take to her. And I do.

At first, I was sad about not knowing what was going on with Mama. Ever since I was little, I have always done whatever is in my power to keep my Mama smiling. My sadness, though, has started to turn into anger because I am realizing that my life is more public than I would like it to be. Whatever is happening to Mama has started to be school gossip.

Wherever I go, I can't get away from people asking me about my Mama. Walking through the hallways of Bringhurst Prep, I overhear nearly everyone talking about her.

And then, there's Vivian.

I see her walking toward me in the hallway. In her hand, there's a folded piece of the pink paper she always uses to pass notes in class.

Oh God, not today!

"This is for you." Vivian smiles as he hands me the letter. I'm confused. Never in my life have Vivian and I been friends; exchanging notes has never been our thing. Even though I'm not buying this act, I still take the note — just in case she really *has* had a change in heart.

Vivian walks away and I unfold the pink paper out of the four, creased squares she has made.

> *"Hey, Safiri. Is your mom dying or something?"*
> *-Vivian*

The words burn a hole through my heart. They also light a fire that I didn't even know I had until now. Even though I usually don't let Vivian know that she has gotten under my skin, I can't help it this time. I see her standing next to the school trophy case. She disgusts me more than ever now, and there is nothing anyone can do to make Vivian Coats worthy of me even looking at her right now. The spirit sign with the words *WARRIOR SPIRIT* that hangs above the school's athletic trophy case is where my eyes land. The red, yellow, and black paint of each letter fuels my anger as if it is some type of tribal war paint. Before I know it, I am marching right toward the center of the gossip circle that Vivian and her minions have formed. I see them laugh as she points toward my direction. My hands begin to sweat as I suddenly begin to feel tired — sick and tired, to be exact, of Vivian and her cruel jokes.

I decide that I need to see it. I need to see the evil in this villain's eyes because even for Vivian, her letter to me is a low blow. As our eyes meet, somehow, I see *Vanessa,* not Vivian. In that moment, it's like I am staring at an evil character that has jumped right off the pages of my yellow notebook. I know this girl — I've probably written about her at least fifteen times in the last year. My hands become hot, then cold. My sweaty palms clench tightly against my fingertips. There is something inside of me that I can no longer control. Looking at Vivian, I can see her laughter turn to fear. She shrinks back from my gaze. I am not afraid of her or her words.

"What do *you* want?" she snaps at me as she flips hair that rests on her right shoulder.

It seems as if, one moment I am looking at her trying to act cool in front of the crowd that has stopped to look at us. The next, she is holding the left side of her face, and the palm of my right hand is stinging from slapping her so hard. I laugh as I cry — not knowing which one I should do. But either way, I feel like I want to do it again.

"Keep my Mama out of your thoughts. We don't need your sympathy."

My voice doesn't sound like my own; in it, I hear something that sounds like Josephine — my Mama. I hear hurt and power all rolled up in one. But I don't hear fear anymore.

Calmly, I walk away, leaving Vivian and the crowd of spectators in the hallway. I feel them all staring at me as I walk toward the front office. But I don't care.

The school secretary, Mrs. Darby, smiles at me the way she always does when I come to the office, but this time, the smile does not last. Her bottom lip curls upward as she puts her hand over her heart and looks at me as if she feels sorry for me.

"Oh Safiri, I'm so sorry, honey," she looks at me and says.

Seeing that I have come straight from the hallway to the front office, there's no way that Mrs. Darby could be talking about what just happened with Vivian.

"What do you mean?" I ask her.

Mrs. Darby's smile suddenly fades, and for some reason she looks terrified — as if I'm a ghost or something.

"Uhm ... do you need help, sweetie?" she asks.

Clearly, she hasn't heard about what I've done. And whatever she was sorry about when I first came in the office is no longer up for discussion.

"I need to speak with the principal, please."

Mama always taught me not to lie. But even after I tell the truth and explain everything to Principal Wesley, I know I am still going to be in trouble once I get home.

Since Mama is still out sick, Mrs. Darby lets me sit with her while I wait for Daddy to pick me up. Since today seems to be the day for crying, I let the tears fall down my cheeks and into my lap. I don't think about getting in trouble, though. I don't even give Vivian another thought. The only thing I want to do is get home and ask questions, questions about Mama that I should have asked well before today.

"Safiri Josephine, are you ready?"

The only person who calls me by both my first and middle name is probably my second favorite person in the world next to Mama — Aunt Annie-Lou. Annabel-Louise is Mama's older sister's real name, but we call her Aunt Annie-Lou for short. She is the type of aunt who always knows what to say and how to say it. She never had children of her own, so the only practice she has with kids is me. Aunt Annie-Lou does things her way. Just like her sister, once she gets her mind set on something, there isn't anything anyone can do to change it, that's for sure.

"Aunt Annie-Lou!" I nearly knock everything off Mrs. Darby's desk when I leap out of my seat towards my auntie.

"Hey, girl," she says, chuckling. "I didn't know you had it in you! Come on. I'm taking you home."

Leave it up to Aunt Annie-Lou to make a joke about the situation. After a few words with Principal Wesley, she signs the clipboard at the front desk to check me out of school. My aunt walks quickly out of the building; so quickly that walking toward her silver Jeep Cherokee, I can barely keep up with her stride. I know I am going to be in lots of trouble when I see Mama and Daddy, but for the moment, being with Aunt Annie-Lou makes everything OK.

I talk so much on the ride home with Aunt Annie-Lou that by the time we pull in the driveway and see Daddy sitting on the back of his truck, there is little left to say.

"Well, little lady, looks like somebody's been waiting for you. Good luck."

Aunt Annie-Lou leans over and kisses me on the cheek.

Daddy opens the passenger door and helps me out of the jeep.

"Thank you, Annie-Lou. We really appreciate this." Daddy's voice comes out low. His usually strong voice doesn't travel farther than the car door.

The look on his face lets me know that whatever conversation I had to have with him and Mama about

Vivian was going to go in a totally different direction than it had with Aunt Annie-Lou.

"Awe, Vance. Don't worry about it. Tell Josie I will call her to work out the

schedule for the next week, too," she replies.

Spending time with my favorite aunt would usually be something to celebrate. But from the looks of things, I'll be lucky if I even *make* it into next week.

Walking into our house, I hear nothing. Daddy hasn't said anything to me at all. He hasn't even asked me about what happened with Vivian.

"Safiri. Can you come here please?"

Mama's soft, trembling voice startles me so much that I forget to take my backpack off at the door like I usually do when I get home from school. The upbeat, high pitch of her voice usually lifts my spirits. Today, however, it sounds so empty and sad that I barely recognize the voice as hers.

With Daddy behind me, I walk slowly toward their room. I am a little scared when I walk in. Usually, Mama jumps on my case about whatever it is I've done before I take two steps past the doorway. Today, though, I make it all the way in the house before even knowing she's home.

Something isn't right.

My heart feels like it's about jump right through my shirt.

"Safiri, sit down, baby. There is something that your Daddy and I need to tell you," Mama says, signaling with her hand for me to sit down.

Sitting in Mama's big recliner that faces the window, I am directly across from my parents' bed. Daddy lowers himself next to Mama; he rests his left hand on her leg as he finds his place next to her. No one smiles. No one laughs. The serious expressions on Mama's and Daddy's faces are enough to make me afraid that the punishment they are about to give me for hitting Vivian will be like nothing they have ever done.

"Mama...Daddy. I'm sorry! I just couldn't take it!"

Fearful, I begin to plead my case. I tell Mama and Daddy exactly what had happened to make me lose my cool with Vivian. Even though I still don't regret it, I start to wonder what mess I have gotten myself into by deciding to finally stand up to Vivian — to actually do something more than just write in my pretty yellow notebook about a make-believe story.

"Safiri. Let's talk about that later," Mama replies. She looks at me with red eyes and I immediately know she has been crying.

"What's going on?" I ask. I dig my fingernails into the back of the chair, the way I have done every time I've sat in this seat while waiting to hear what my punishment will be for whatever wrong I've done. Right now, though, I feel more like a criminal waiting for the judge to hand down the prison sentence.

"Safiri, your Mama is going to be taking a little more time off of work to get some rest," Daddy says.

There is no trace of the smile that he usually wears when he's around Mama, and this scares me. I am confused, as Daddy talks. As long as I have known my Mama, she has only missed this much work once in my entire life — when my grandmother died.

"Is something wrong?" I ask.

I can hear my voice tremble. The inside of my hands have started to sweat. I feel a knot in the pit of my stomach — it doesn't seem like the usual knot that comes when I know I'm in trouble. This feeling is somehow letting me know that something is terribly wrong.

As Daddy opens his mouth to talk again, Mama interrupts.

"I'm sick, Safiri."

By the look on Daddy's face, I can tell that he hadn't exactly planned to tell me the full truth. I know my Daddy. To him, I will always be his precious and fragile little girl. Mama, the one who has always promised to tell me the truth, on the other hand, keeps her end of the bargain; she gives me the honest answer no matter what.

"What do you mean, Mama?" I ask.

The only thing I can manage to do is hold my breath, waiting to hear what she's going to say next.

"Baby, I won't be working at Bringhurst Prep anymore."

As Mama ends her sentence, she looks into my eyes, as if she is speaking directly to my heart. At least that's what it feels like. Hearing the news shocks the breath out of me. I look for words — words that will help me ask the right questions, whatever they may be.

"Why not, Mama? Where are you going to work?"

"I'm not going to be working anywhere this year, Safiri," she replies.

The news seems to be getting worse with every word Mama says. Suddenly, I begin to long for my Mama in a way that the four-year-old me used to do before Mama went to work at Bringhurst Preparatory Academy. I want to jump in her lap, tell Mama I love her, and listen to her tell me that everything is going to be okay. My feet don't move, though; my lips stay shut.

"Safiri, honey, Daddy and I are fighting this thing — God knows we aren't giving up, but ..."

Mama pauses and looks me in the eyes, gently holding my arms at the elbows. Her trembling voice, along with the tears that are flowing down her face, pierce me. For the first time in my entire life, I see my strong Mama look afraid.

"Baby, what I am trying to tell you is not easy to say, but I have always been very honest with you, and it's time that you know what is going on."

"Mama," I whisper. "You're scaring me. What's going on?"

"Safiri, honey. I can barely explain this thing myself," she begins. "The best way I can put it is that my body has gotten a little confused."

I'm breathing so hard out of fear that I can barely hear Mama's voice. I hold my breath as she continues to speak.

"The part of my immune system that is supposed to keep me healthy is attacking everything. My body just can't keep up. Everything has been hurting me, Safiri. I'm not myself. I'm..."

As Mama stops speaking, her eyes begin to blink fast. I can tell that she is trying to be strong — trying not to cry in front of me. Her sweaty palms grip both of my elbows; her voice is now trembling. I can tell that she's rehearsed this speech — the same way she has rehearsed her pineapple sugar speech. This time, though, she is giving me a life lesson that it seems neither of us wants to learn.

"Safiri, the doctors say that there may not be much more time for me to live."

Whatever Mama's lips are saying, I can no longer hear. She's babbling and stuttering in a way that I've never heard her do before. For the first time in my life, I am watching Mama struggle to find the right words — words to tell me that she's dying.

"Baby, I don't want you to give up on me! Your father and I are trying everything. That's why I haven't been back to work. After all of this time, nothing has worked yet. The doctors have said there is nothing more that they can do but…"

I try to stand, but I can't. My legs are locked at the knees. Even in my seat, they buckle a little bit, but still don't move. I try to find words to say that can fight back…words that would turn everything that Mama is saying into a big lie. Suddenly, I have a thought that makes even this moment, worse.

Vivian was right. Mama is going to die.

There is nothing left to say. I cover my ears, thinking that will make the bad news stop. I close my eyes as tightly as I possibly can and plug my ears with my index fingers. But I can still hear Mama's voice pleading with me to listen — her desperate voice sounds about a hundred miles away.

"Sugar, you have got to listen to me!" she cries.

Daddy reaches out to put his arms around me, but I pull away. I don't want anyone to touch me. Tears begin to well up in my eyes, but I fight them, too.

I feel hurt and betrayed at the same time. Honestly, I cannot tell one from the other. News like this isn't something that just happens overnight. I am the last person to know and I'm pissed. Being too sick to work is one thing, but dying? That's totally different, and I had a right to know.

It's all starting to make sense: Rev. Bingham and his prayer *and* Mrs. Darby telling me how sorry she was. How *dare* Mama and Daddy! Everyone knows! They told everyone — everyone but me.

Still in disbelief, I turn and face Mama. Her lips are still moving. I don't want to listen, though. I don't want to accept or believe anything that she has to say at this point but I've been in the dark too long. So, I take my hands from my ears in time to hear her explain.

"I'm at the point where I just want to take time to live – to live out the rest of my days here with you and your Daddy."

I interrupt, "What do you mean the rest of your days, Mama?" My voice is louder and much stronger than I had intended, but I cannot control it. "You just said you aren't giving up!"

Mama continues to speak. "My time, now, is more precious than ever. There is so much that I want to share with you, Safiri..."

I cannot believe I am actually living a moment like this. My Mama – the one who has always loved and cared for me no matter what, is going to die, and there is nothing anyone can do about it. As I jump up to run out of the room, Mama's soft hand catches me by the sleeve. I turn to tell her to let me go, but when I glance at her frail hand — a hand that seems to be grasping for her own life, no words come out. I just stand there and stare — I stare at the woman who carried me in her womb for thirty-nine weeks and six and a half days, as she always reminds me anytime I get sassy and short-tempered with her. I stare at the woman who always helps me with my homework; the beautiful woman who, when I am sick, crawls into my germ-filled bed and snuggles up close to me, not even worrying about catching what I have. I helplessly stand there, looking at my dying Mama.

Our eyes meet. My knees become weak. I feel myself begin to fall. Just like a dramatic scene out of a movie, Mama grabs me before I can hit the floor. She pulls me closely towards her chest. I scream and cry as I lie across her frail body.

I beg her to tell me she is lying about everything. She rocks me back and forth while I'm paralyzed in disbelief. The person whom I have always been able to count on to make me laugh and smile will be leaving me forever.

I simply can't take it. I can't stand to look at Mama another second. It simply hurts too much. I grab my backpack and run out of her and Daddy's room.

"Safiri! Safiri!"

I hear Mama and Daddy call me, but I don't turn around. All I want to do is run as fast as I can to wherever my legs will take me.

I dash into the kitchen and head for the back door. Just as I reach for the doorknob, I trip on the kitchen mat, lose my balance, and crash to the floor.

It is all too much: the bad news, the fall, *and* my life. I can't do anything but lie with my face to the floor, crying. How could this happen? I am twelve-years-old and my mother is dying! I feel like somebody, somewhere, is punishing me for every bad thing that I have ever done in my life.

"I'm sorry," I whisper, still lying on the floor and pulling my backpack in towards my chest. Who I am talking to, I have no clue. Somewhere in my mind, though, I figure that if I am being punished, then maybe an apology will make everything all right and take Mama's illness away.

My mind is racing. I feel like a big rock has been dropped on top of my shoulders. Somehow, I find the strength to get up from my fall and go up to my room. I reach for my yellow notebook, grab the red pen sitting on my nightstand, plop down across my bed, and wait for the words to come as they always have. I place the pen to the first line of the paper and wait for the magic to come and take me away from the horrible nightmare that has just unfolded downstairs with Mama and Daddy. Nothing comes, though. Nothing at all.

With my hands covering my face, I begin to cry. Keeping my eyes open, I stare into the darkness of my palms. My tears trickle down my face and onto the empty page of my notebook. The only care in the world that I have is how to make Mama's sickness go away. Those doctors have to be wrong. It also doesn't seem right that they can just give up on Mama like that. That just doesn't seem fair. Surely, Mama doesn't really have to die. None of any of this makes sense to me, and honestly, I don't want it to — not if it doesn't change the fact that Mama is dying and there is nothing neither I, nor anyone else, can do about it.

chapter 4:

MY MOTHER'S DAUGHTER

I can remember when my grandmother passed away two weeks after my seventh birthday. That was the first time anyone that I knew had ever died. I cried a lot when Daddy broke the news to me.

I loved Gran so much, and learning that she would never be coming back was hard for me; not just because I lost her forever, but because that was the day I saw a change in Mama that I had never seen before. It seemed like the day Gran died was the day Mama stopped smiling. I began to worry that the smile that always seemed to be perfectly painted across Mama's face would never return. I got scared that Mama was going to be sad forever.

She walked around for days with her eyes filled with tears ready to fall at a moment's notice.

"Daddy, is Mama going to be OK?" I asked.

"Just give her time, Safiri. She loves you very much. She just needs time to grieve, sweetheart."

"What is grieve?" I innocently asked.

Mama was always the one who knew how to explain things to me. She would make sure to answer all of my questions, no matter how much I asked her. Daddy, though, didn't have the same patience as Mama; probably because I had never really asked him much of anything since Mama was always around. With Daddy, things were just the way they were — no extra discussion was really needed. When he spoke, I listened, and that's all there ever was to it at that point.

That day, he tried the best he could to give me the definition of a word to which he usually never gave a second thought.

"Well, Safiri, when you lose someone close to you, it can make you very sad," he said. "Sad enough that you don't want to live your life the way you did when that person was here with you."

I took what he gave me as an answer to my question and panicked. His words seemed so final and so matter of fact.

"So Mama is going to die now?" I cried.

Daddy sighed and waved his hands toward my question. He then pressed his left hand against his brow as he looked for another explanation.

"No, No, No, Safiri. Your Mama isn't dying!" he exclaimed. "She is just figuring out how to live now that her Mama is gone."

Even though I didn't really understand what Daddy was saying, I made enough sense of it to know that Mama's grief wouldn't last forever.

I was relieved by his answer. Daddy went on to tell me that the best way that I could help Mama figure things out was to be a "big girl." As a seven-year-old, being a "big girl" just meant that I wouldn't wait for Mama to run my bathwater the way I usually did. Instead, I would do it myself. I also made sure to clean up my room without her having to tell me to.

In the days following Gran's funeral, Daddy took me to school and picked me up while Mama stayed home to rest and grieve. Even though she was resting, I know she did more crying than anything else. Daddy even took over making sure I had lunch. He did two solid days of peanut butter and jelly sandwiches before he realized he was in over his head.

"Safiri, honey, you're going to buy your lunch at school for a little while. Is that alright with you?" he asked as we walked out of the house one morning.

Trying to keep my cool, I did my best to hold back my smile, but that didn't really work.

"Yes, sir," I replied with a grin.

Every morning before kissing Mama goodbye, I would get two dollars: a dollar and seventy-five cents for lunch and twenty-five cents for apple juice.

If Mama and Daddy let me, I would have no problem drinking apple juice all day, every day. So, even though I didn't have the special lunches that Mama always made for me, I could survive off apple juice each day if I needed to.

One morning before school, I walked into the kitchen to find Mama holding my lunch kit, crying. Her chin was resting on Daddy's chest while he held her and kissed her forehead.

"I'm trying, Vance...I'm trying so hard, but I miss her so much," she sobbed.

"I know, baby. I know," Daddy whispered back.

I remember, that day, going quietly into the kitchen, where Mama and Daddy were, and picking up the mess of chips, bread, and turkey meat that Mama had let fall from my lunch bag. They didn't even hear me come in.

"It's okay, Mama. I can eat lunch at school again today. Don't worry," I said, holding the pile of food I had picked up off the floor from around Mama and Daddy's feet.

That day, I made the biggest sacrifice I probably ever made as a seven-year-old — I decided to give up my apple juice just for Mama. I made a plan to continue to work in the extra quarter each day from Daddy, but I stopped buying apple juice all together because I wanted to do something special for Mama to make her feel better. I missed Mama's smile so much that I was willing to try anything to help her get it back — even if it meant drinking water from the water fountain during lunch.

Every Friday has always been Dollar Store Day at Bringhurst Prep. So, the next Friday, after five days of giving up my apple juice at lunch, I was so excited that I finally had enough money to buy one of the prizes with the five quarters I had saved. Even though the school store was nothing more than a small storage closet that Principal Wesley had turned into a home for every kind of sticker and pencil bag a little kid could ever imagine, it felt like a shopping mall to me because there were so many choices.

I searched and searched for the perfect pick-me-up for Mama. The teachers only gave us three minutes to make our selections in the store, so I knew I had to be quick. Still, I wanted to make sure that whatever I chose was smile-worthy for Mama.

From the corner of my eye, a pretty yellow, green, and white striped book with the word "diary" written on it caught my attention. I knew that anything yellow would be a win. I reached down to pick up the journal, carefully placing one hand on the spiral, and the other on the back of the diary so that I didn't accidentally rip it.

This is the perfect gift for Mama, I thought!

As I handled the notebook, I noticed the price tag: $1.50.

"One minute left, Safiri," my teacher, Mrs. Franklin, announced.

I clutched the diary tightly in my hands and walked toward the table where the teacher collected all of the money for the store.

"Did you find anything good, Safiri?" Mrs. Franklin asked.

"This is what I want — well, it's what I need to make my Mama feel better. Daddy said she's grieving over Gran, and I want to help her smile again, like she used to. Do I have enough?"

I've never been great with numbers — even as a seven-year-old first grader. I was clueless about how much

I actually had. Unsure and nervous, I handed Mrs. Franklin my five quarters.

My teacher looked down at me, and back at the diary. I got scared that she was going to tell me that I didn't have enough money. Time had run out, and if I didn't buy something, I was going to be forced to wait until next Friday to come back to the store.

Mrs. Franklin smiled at me as she placed the quarters in the moneybox that kept all of the change from the school store. "You know what, hun? It looks like I marked this with the wrong price. It's only a dollar and twenty-five cents — that's five quarters and you've got it! Your Mama is really going to love it."

I could barely contain my excitement. I took the notebook from Mrs. Franklin and put it in my backpack. For the rest of the day, the only thing that I could think about was giving Mama her present.

I have never been good at keeping secrets but that day, I waited until dinnertime to give Mama her present.

"Mama, I got this for you."

I handed her the notebook that I had bought from the school store for five quarters.

I began to tell her about how we had to write in our journals every day at school and how my teacher said writing helps you feel better.

"Maybe you can write about Gran in this diary every day so that you can feel better even though she died. After that, maybe you will be happy and smile again. I don't think Gran would want you to be sad." I told Mama.

Mama's eyes filled with tears. She didn't say anything to me — nothing at all. All she did was hug me so tightly that I thought I was going to turn blue from not being able to breathe. But I didn't complain. I just waited for Mama to let go.

"Thank you, baby," Mama said as she wiped the tears that had fallen down her cheeks.

"You're welcome, Mama."

As we started our short drive home, for the first time in the seven days since Gran had died, Mama turned on the radio and started singing. Strangely enough, her smile - the one that I had almost foolishly thought would never return, slowly found its way back to her lips. To this day, I still feel those five quarters were the best I have ever spent in my life.

Now, however, it was going to take more than a few quarters to make things right, not just for Mama, but for me.

After Gran died, the entire family began to wonder who would keep everyone together the way she always had. Besides, every holiday, all of us would travel from our homes, from near and far, to the house where Mama grew up just to feast on Gran's delicious meals. The amount of food that would cover Gran's dining room table made it difficult to believe that Gran had cooked everything herself. But she always did. It was hard to imagine that there was anyone in the family who could do things quite the way Gran had done for so many years.

One Saturday morning shortly after Gran's funeral, Mama asked me and Daddy a question that would change our holiday tradition forever.

"How would you guys feel if I hosted the family's Thanksgiving dinner this year?"

Daddy and I didn't bother to stop chewing, but somehow our eyes met with the same "oh boy" expression.

"Sweetheart, that is a big job."

"I know, Vance, but somebody has to keep this family together. Mama worked so hard to make sure that we always came together during holidays. The least I can do is host Thanksgiving for our family," she said.

For as long as I had lived, I had never seen Daddy win a debate with Mama, and I knew that I wasn't about to see anything new while sitting at the table that day. Excusing myself from the table, I knew exactly what was going to happen: Mama would tell Daddy how she felt about family, Daddy would come back with some logical explanation as to why hosting Mama's entire family would not be the best idea, and then Mama would do it anyway.

Five months later, my entire family, every last cousin, aunt, and uncle, was standing around our dining room table as Daddy said grace and blessed Mama's first big Thanksgiving meal.

Ever since Mama took on the role of Thanksgiving chef five years ago, she has taken the tradition on as if she had been doing it all along. Every year, she props herself up in the kitchen two nights before Thanksgiving day, seasoning the turkey, baking macaroni and cheese, kneading the dough for homemade rolls, and baking cakes. It is usually around this time that she complains about how small our kitchen is and always makes Daddy promise that one day, he will build her a dream house with a kitchen the size of a small shack. Every year, Daddy laughs and promises to build Mama her dream house as soon as we win the lottery. Both she and I know that he's never even bought a ticket, but we always laugh and pretend to keep our fingers crossed.

One thing that I think we have all learned about Mama is that she is a woman who knows how to bring people together – especially with her cooking. Thanksgiving, now, has become her favorite holiday. She has traded in her early Christmas shopping sprees for coupon cutting, bargain scouting, and exchanging new recipes with the cooking club that she joined after hosting Thanksgiving for the first time.

"We don't give Thanksgiving enough credit," she complains. "It seems like the only things folks get excited about come with shopping bags and credit card bills!"

Because of Mama and the big deal that she always makes out of it, I think Thanksgiving has secretly become my favorite holiday. There is something about the combination of no school, family, and all-you-can-eat home-cooked food that gives me a feeling I can't really describe. About two years ago, I decided that at least three days before turkey day, I would only eat dinner – no breakfast, no lunch, and no snacks. Just dinner. I wanted to make sure that my stomach had enough room for me to eat as much as my little heart desired when our Thanksgiving feast happened.

It's already October now, and I haven't heard Mama make any mention about Thanksgiving. Usually by now, she makes sure folks don't forget that she is counting on them to make Thanksgiving special with their presence around the dinner table. How can she talk about Thanksgiving this year, though? She doesn't even know if she will be here next week.

I know that Mama loves Thanksgiving, but even she admits that this year, she is too tired to cook. There is no way that Daddy would even think about taking on a Thanksgiving dinner, either. Mama is the glue of our entire family and has been for a very long time. All of our family members look forward to coming over to our house for the holiday, not only to eat mama's famous cooking, but also to spend time as a family, recounting old times, and retelling childhood events to the younger generation. Without Mama, however, none of this can happen. Without Mama, there will be no Thanksgiving for our family this year.

Suddenly, a thought jumps into my mind and a plan starts to unfold. *I* need to step in and do something. For as long as I can remember, Mama has always made sure everything is perfect for Thanksgiving day — all the way down to the special plates hidden away in the cupboard that she only takes down during the holidays. Maybe now, it is finally time to do everything Mama has ever taught me about folding napkins, setting the table, and using the right glasses to keep with our Thanksgiving tradition. No matter what it takes, I am going to make this Thanksgiving the best one Mama has ever had.

chapter 5:
GREEN LINES

This time, I am the one who will be using the little yellow pineapple address book that is tucked away in Mama's nightstand. I don't know everyone in the book, the way Mama seems to, but I don't care.

Since Mama hasn't been working, she has had time to be even more thoughtful than she already is. Before now, you could pretty much rest assured that no matter how far removed an uncle, cousin, or any member our family is, Mama knows how to find them. Tons of phone calls have come in over the years from folks thanking her for those random care packages of baked goodies that she sends, along with notes that simply read, "*I am just thinking about you.*"

Now, Mama spends her days writing notes to as many family members as she can. She has even started to make the stationery paper that she usually saves for special occasions the regular choice for her letters. Our kitchen table is now a sea of envelopes, stamps, and pens of every color that Mama uses to handwrite the letters – each one written with the same care she would give if she were writing to the President of The United States. She takes her time, to make sure that no detail is missed. Name by name, Mama moves through each line of her yellow, pineapple covered address book just to brighten someone's day and with a few special words.

Since Mama has been working on her letters to family members, getting a hold of her address book is a simple walk to the kitchen table where she writes her letters. On top of her big stack of stationery sits the address book.

From the way the yellow, pineapple cover barely clings to the wire spiral, I can tell that the address book has seen better days. There is no way of truly knowing how old it is, but the dingy, faded pages let me know that the notebook probably has more years behind it than I did.

I see that certain names have a green line drawn through them. There are only a few pages that don't have any green marks on them, so there is no pattern to follow. With my finger, I trace each name for what seems like one hundred times, trying to recall each one that wears the solid green line through it. I start to grow impatient with myself while trying to solve the green line puzzle of Mama's book.

Knowing that there's a chance that I may get in trouble for going through Mama's things, I set the yellow, pineapple notebook down in front of her anyway.

"Mama, why do you have lines through names in this notebook?"

She looks at me for a moment, as if she is trying to find the right words to put me in my place for snooping around in her junk draw again. All she does is look me right in my eyes and sit back in her chair.

"Why, Mama?" I ask impatiently

Mama lets out a deep sigh. "Those people have passed away, baby."

I almost wish that she wouldn't have given me an answer at all. Thinking about Mama and death at the same time makes me want to scream and cry at the same time. But it's my fault; I asked the question, but I hadn't been ready for *that* answer. My mind starts running, again.

I don't want Mama to be another green line in that yellow, pineapple address book.

Without saying another word, I leave the little pineapple address book sitting on the table in front of Mama and head straight to my room.

Making a list of everything I ever remember Mama cooking for Thanksgiving is harder than I thought it would be. After cornbread dressing, and turkey, I take a minute to close my eyes and picture the big plate of food that I always pile up right after we say "amen" at the end of the Thanksgiving grace.

Rolls, ham, homemade cranberry sauce, green beans, and macaroni.

The list begins to grow longer and longer. By the time I get to the end of the page, I am amazed at how much food Mama cooks in such a short amount of time! This year, though, would be different.

My plan is to call those on the list and ask them to do their part in making this year's Thanksgiving come together. We will still have it at our house, but Mama will not be doing any of the cooking. This year, our entire family will give Mama a break. I figure if every family brings just one dish, everything on our Thanksgiving menu will be covered.

The first call I make is to Aunt Annie-Lou. After having the small talk that we usually start every phone conversation with, I waste no time telling her about my idea to host Thanksgiving dinner. As I explain my plan to Aunt Annie-Lou, she stays silent until I finish speaking. I get a little worried because I don't hear any sound coming from her end of the phone line.

"Hello? Are you still there, Aunt Annie-Lou?"

"You have determination, just like your Mama, child," she whispers.

My heart nearly skips a beat at the thought of having any amount of strength that could compare with Mama's.

Without hesitation, Aunt Annie-Lou offers to call half of the names in the address book. I quickly accept her offer because I only see some of my family members once a year at Thanksgiving so I don't really know them well.

"You just use your Mama's address book to take care of the family we have around here, Safiri. I will do the rest," says Aunt Annie-Lou.

Once that part is settled, I begin to read the Thanksgiving menu to her. As I read, Aunt Annie-Lou comments on things that need to be added or taken away for this year's feast. She also explains to me whom she feels will be the best person to ask for each dish.

"Honey, if we're going to get it done, it needs to be good. There is no need asking your cousin Marie to make a turkey if she can't even make toast," she jokes.

My aunt and I work together to figure out how to get every item off our food list and onto the Thanksgiving table. We then decide to keep our little plan a secret. It will be tough making sure that no one in the family tells Mama or Daddy about our plan. We both agree, though, that this particular surprise is well worth the try.

"Girl, your Mama and Daddy are gonna hit the floor when everybody comes strolling through their door," Aunt Annie-Lou declares.

My excitement starts to take over and I try to hurry my aunt off of the phone.

"Safiri,"

"Yes, Aunt Annie-Lou?" I reply.

"I'm so proud of you, sweetie. Your mother is going to be so happy."

With that, I hang up with my Aunt and dial Cousin Avery's number.

chapter 6:

MAKING MEMORIES

The cool, November air always lets me know that Thanksgiving is near; it's one of the first signs that the cruel, southern heat will soon give way to the cold weather the holiday season brings.

Besides thinking about Mama and her sickness, my plans for Thanksgiving have stayed on my mind. Lying in bed this morning, I'm thankful that today is the last day of school before Thanksgiving break. Now, I will finally be able to concentrate on Operation Thanksgiving — otherwise known as my plan to bring the family together without Mama and Daddy having a clue.

"Good morning, baby. Are you awake?"

My thoughts are so loud that I don't even notice Mama enter my room. I'm not expecting early morning company, so her voice startles me so much that I nearly fall out of my bed. She is looking down at me and smiling the way I remember her doing when I was a little girl. Waking up to see Mama smiling at me is one of the best feelings in the world.

"Yes, Mama. Are you okay?" I ask sitting up in bed.

A sudden flash of light nearly makes me fall to the floor.

"Smile, girl! You're on camera!"

Mama pats my knee, and signals with her hand for me to scoot over. As she crawls in my bed, I can see her face frown in pain at each moment, but she doesn't stop until she is tucked under the cover with me.

"Let's take one of those selfie things, Safiri! Come on! One...two...three...CHEESE!"

Posing for the camera first thing in the morning isn't exactly on my to-do list, but hearing Mama say "cheese" like I'm five years old is hard to resist.

As Mama and I lean together to take our picture, I see that the square screen inside of the hard, yellow case is not just a camera.

"It's a phone!" I gasp. "When did you get a new one, Mama?"

"Well…it's not exactly mine, honey. Let me show you something."

Since Mama has never been good with "anything that beeps", as she calls it, I'm amazed how she is working so well with the phone in her hand. She opens the photo gallery app, slides her finger across the smartphone's screen, and hands the yellow device over to me.

"Check this out! We look cute, don't we?" she asks playfully.

I look at the photo, but don't see the one Mama and I just took. Instead, I see my friends — Maisy, Kimberly, and Eileen, posing together with Mama.

"Guess what, Safiri!" Mama exclaims before I can ask about the picture.

I try to guess *what,* but after her third, "Nuh-uh," I give up.

"You're not going to school today!"

Even when I am sick, if I'm not *sick enough* like Mama calls it, I'm going to school. So hearing Mama's news is more than just a surprise. It's a miracle that I nearly find hard to believe.

"I called the school and let them know you wouldn't be there today," she continues. "Besides, what really goes on in a school on the last day before a long break? Your Daddy has already gone to pick up your homework so you won't miss anything."

Never in my life have I ever heard Mama talk about school this way. For as long as I can remember, it has always been second nature to get up and go to school no matter what time of year it is. Mama has even drug me to work with her when the school was closed.

"There may be no school today, Safiri, but that library is open," she always reminds me.

"You don't need a teacher there for you to learn something — pick up a book!"

This time, though, there are no meetings to attend; there's no library time for me. My disbelief disappears as I give Mama a big hug.

"One more thing, girl!"

Already, surprised, I turn to see what else Mama could possibly have up her sleeve.

"You may want to get dressed, now. Maisy, Kimberly and Eileen are outside of your door waiting on us. You don't want the *best* picture on your new phone to be the one *I* took with them this morning. Come on in, girls!"

"Mama!" I scream as the shrills of my friends match mine. Everyone jumps on my bed in excitement of a whole day away from school together.

"Well now, let's get this party started, girls!" she exclaims. Mama does her best to jump up and do a little dance. Her hips barely move, though, and watching her throw up both hands in the air to the imaginary rhythm in her head makes me giggle. Looking at Mama wiggle around, and hearing her laughter fill my bedroom, along with Maisy, Kimberly and Eileen's, gives me hope that things can one day go back to the way they were before she got sick — no matter what the doctors have told her. Miracles happen all the time, and I desperately want one now to keep Mama alive.

As she turns to leave, my feet can't help but jump out of bed to go and hug her.

"Thank you, Mama. Thank you so much."

She leans over to whisper in my ear, "Have fun with your girls today, Safiri. It's just you and me for the rest of the break. We're going to have our own girl time!"

"Okay, Mama," I reply as she walk out of my room.

I spend most of the day laughing at Maisy's jokes and hearing the latest school gossip from Eileen and Kimberly. They all help me learn how to use my new phone and do their part in quickly filling the camera with pictures of all four of us.

As the day winds down, we turn on the television and channel surf through all of the talk shows until we find something worth keeping on just for noise. Kimberly and I take to playing on my new phone, while Maisy and Eileen raid my closet for something to wear to the mall over Thanksgiving break.

I can't help but think of how between the four of us, no one has mentioned anything about Mama or her sickness. We all know that if Josephine Fields were well, then *all* of us would be in school today. Outside of gossiping about Mama's substitute teacher, though, between the friends who share everything with one another, not one word is spoken about how she is doing.

To be honest, neither of us has ever had to think about the possibility of one of our parents dying. What exactly do you say to a girl whose mom has an illness that can't be cured? Is Maisy supposed to make a joke about it? Should Eileen pretend that she knows what I am going through? The truth is that I haven't really known what to say to anyone about what's going on. How do I start? What words could possibly tell the full story of what I'm feeling? Mama is the reason that Maisy, Kimberly and Eileen are here with me right now, and there is no doubt in my mind that she made this girls' day possible just to make sure that despite everything, I'm okay. That's just how thoughtful Mama is. She's always putting everyone else before herself.

"Guys...I...I...."

My words don't come fast enough and before I know it, I can't stop myself from crying.

Maisy sprints from the closet, kneels beside my legs, and hugs me around my knees as Kimberly smooths down the edges of my hairline to comfort me. Eileen stands in front of me and wipes my tears as quickly as they fall.

"Safiri…it…it's going to be okay." Eileen says quietly.

We sit and cry together for what seems like hours. Finally, everything that I've been feeling comes out to listening ears. We talk until there's nothing else that could be said to let me know that my friends are my sisters who are there for me through everything — even this.

"We'll be here for you, girl. Just call us if when you need us, okay Safiri?" Kimberly requests.

"Okay."

"Friends forever, ya'll" Maisy says, as she raises her hand from my knee.

Kimberly, Eileen and I each place one hand on top of Maisy's the same way we have always done when we want to make a promise to each other.

"Friends, forever," we agree in unison.

The Friday sun goes down, and my friends leave with their parents one by one. I've never had a day like today — especially on a school day. By far, between hanging out with my best friends in the world and getting a new cell phone, this day is going down in the Safiri history book.

"Did you have fun, baby? Ya'll didn't even need me for most of the day. Can't your Mama get invited to the party, too?"

As usual, Mama laughs at her own sense of humor. Before she finishes her round of laughter, however, I wrap my arms around her and give her the biggest hug I have given her since the day she and Daddy told me how sick she is.

"Thank you, Mama. It was perfect. I love you."

"I love you too, baby," she replies.

Over the weekend, we spend the hours of our days talking about just about everything. Some things, I have already heard before. Other stories that Mama shares are from her childhood — things that she has never told me about her life.

"Safiri," she begins, "there are so many things that I want to share with you. I have always taught you to be thankful for what you have and I am so happy and thankful to be able to spend this time with you."

Mama is always looking on the bright side of things. Right now though, the anger that I felt the day she and Daddy told me about her illness, begins to come back to me faster than I can control. Hearing her talk about the last moments of her life bring a nervous feeling to my heart. Her thankfulness, now, suddenly annoys me. How can she be thankful for anything when she is dying?

I've never been good at hiding what I'm thinking, especially not from Mama. Between my facial expression and body language, it's not hard to figure out how I'm feeling about whatever is in front of me. Only Mama's pats on the back snap me out of my angry thoughts.

"There is pineapple sugar even now, baby. If we spend this time being upset and mad, then we won't have time to enjoy it."

I have to admit that she's right. I *do* spend more time thinking about losing Mama than actually enjoying her while she is here with me. But even though Mama seems to be at peace with dying, I'm not at peace with her leaving me forever. I want to keep hope that somehow, Mama's sickness will disappear. Until that time comes, though, if Mama is being taken from me, then every moment is going to have to count. Saturday's conversations with Mama begin where Friday's end. For the next few days, we spend hours in each other's company. Every night, we talk about details of Mama's childhood and other parts of her life. She shares with me the things she regrets as well as the moments she cherishes.

It feels more like we are best friends than mother and daughter — especially as Mama starts talking about love. After church on Sunday, we decide to get right back in our pajamas and watch every movie about true love that Mama has in her movie collection.

Mama stops every love story we watch about a thousand times, and adds to the list of "rules" for falling in love that she wants me to always remember. She shares that it was Daddy, the nerdy boy from her school, who taught her that sometimes, love comes in unexpected packages. Normally, I would cringe at even the thought of taking advice about boys from Mama. But, the reality that she won't be around to help me figure love out when the time comes helps me enjoy every lesson.

"You won't ever be able to say that your Mama didn't tell you about boys, girl!"

As we talk from Monday to Wednesday, Mama and I laugh more than we cry. As she speaks, my eyes become glued to her every move. I study her as she moves her hands backwards and forwards in sync with her words. I begin to realize how quickly Mama's body has changed. Her already petite frame has gotten so skinny that she can barely fit any of her clothes. The long, thick hair that she has always worn in loose curls is now pulled into a small bun on top of her head each day. Yet, her beauty shines through. Mama's happy-spirited nature makes her beauty even more special to me, especially now.

Suddenly, Mama stops talking. Her face frowns with what appears to me to be pain. I can tell that she is trying hard to hide her expression from me, but I know that Mama is hurting.

"Mama's tired, sugar. Let's pick up again tomorrow," she whispers softly. "I need to rest now."

"Okay, Mama," I reply. "Do you need anything?"

"No, baby. I'm sorry for ruining our special time together today. I wish things were different, you know."

Mama's apology pierces my heart like a poison sword from one of the stories in my book. For a little while, I had forgotten about Mama being sick. It has been so long since I've had time to simply spend with her, and if there is one thing I know, I'm better just from our time together. There is no way that Mama should ever feel as if she ruined anything.

I look Mama straight in the eye and whisper, "You're the best, Mama. I love you."

"I love you too, Safiri. Thank you for being who you are."

After pulling the cover over Mama, I leave her room so that she can sleep. There is nothing peaceful about the way that I feel seeing my Mama in pain right now. I imagine that it must be hard for her not to be able to do things that she is so used to doing without getting tired. I know that the thing she loves to do the most, cook a big meal for her favorite holiday has been on her mind, because lately, she has started apologizing to Daddy and me for not being able to have a big Thanksgiving dinner this year.

Seeing Mama so down makes my Thanksgiving surprise even more important to me. It's starting to get difficult not to spoil the surprise. My full-time task has become worrying about our Thanksgiving dinner for Mama.

"Aunt Annie-Lou!" I whisper into the telephone. "Is everybody still coming?"

"Sugar, everybody is here. You just do your part. We will do the rest," she assures me the night before Thanksgiving.

I am nervous but excited all at the same time. I can't believe that my plan is working. All I have to do now is make sure that Mama and Daddy are dressed for the occasion tomorrow. I know I have to figure out something fast, or else everyone will show up tomorrow all dressed up while Mama and Daddy would barely have on anything more than their pajamas! At this point, there is no time for a big plan. All I can do is ask.

"Mama, I was thinking," I begin. "I know that we are not having anything special tomorrow, but I was wondering if we can get dressed up, like we always do, even though we are going out for Thanksgiving dinner."

Waiting for her response, I know that there is a chance that the tale I'm telling won't fly. It is almost bedtime and I am out of ideas. Mama has been in bed for most of the day and has been complaining about not feeling like doing much of anything tomorrow. I would be lucky if she even agrees to get out of bed tomorrow.

"Okay, sugar." Mama agrees without hesitation. "There's no need for us looking the way I feel!"

I can't believe it! Without thinking, I jump in her bed to hug her and let out a big, "*Yes!*" flailing my hands in the air. The look Mama gives me out of the corner of her eye lets me know that my excitement is disturbing her peace. It is also a look that tells me I only have a few seconds to exit her room or else she might change her mind.

As I run down the hallway to my room, I know that operation Thanksgiving is well underway.

chapter 7:
A FAMILY OF SURPRISES

I love surprises. Everyone in my family knows that. Each year, I try to outdo myself with the gifts that I give to Mama and Daddy for their birthdays. There was the one time when I saved my allowance for six months to send Mama to a spa, even though by month three, I broke down and told her what I was doing because I simply couldn't keep the secret. Daddy could barely believe it last year when I found an exact copy of the old superhero lunch box that he always talked about using as a kid. Never in my entire life have I ever attempted a surprise as big as this one, though. Planning Mama's Thanksgiving dinner is well out of my league.

It is barely five o'clock in the morning now and I'm wide-awake because in about six hours, my entire family will walk through our door with everything from a turkey to collard greens. I begin to imagine everything on the list all spread out on the dining room table with Mama giving me an approving smile. The rolls, glazed ham, cornbread dressing, and all of the sides carve a place for themselves in my mind as I run through the Thanksgiving list one last time.

As my mind moves on to the dessert table, I can almost taste the sweet potato, apple, and pecan pies that will sit right next to the tea cakes that Aunt Annie-Lou will bring. Even in my mind, the view of the entire table is perfect.

Suddenly, I realize that something is missing from my mind's Thanksgiving table. It doesn't take long before the answer hits me like a hammer on a nail's head. I panic as I realize that I had covered every Thanksgiving dinner item with Aunt Annie Lou — every item, that is, except Mama's pineapple sugar cake!

Glancing at the clock, I begin to panic. How could I forget something as important as the pineapple sugar cake? Tears begin to fall down my cheeks. I feel like have somehow managed to ruin my own Thanksgiving surprise.

Crying, I begin to think about how I can undo this mistake. The only person in the world with the recipe is Mama. The only thing I can remember about the cake is how I have sat in the kitchen and watched her mix the six eggs with the two green measuring cups of flour and how she creams two sticks of butter before she mixes it with two yellow measuring cups of sugar.

Wait a minute, I think to myself.

Closing my eyes, I imagine myself in the kitchen with Mama during preparation time for every Thanksgiving I can remember. I focus on all of the things I have seen spread out on the counter year after year. I see the measuring cups, spoons, the mixer, and everything that Mama has ever used for the cake, right down to the vanilla extract.

I scramble for a pencil and paper and scribble down ingredients as quickly as they come to mind. I am not sure if this is going to work, but I immediately know what has to be done to make this day perfect: I will have to make the pineapple sugar cake myself!

Taking the recipe that I've just written down from my memory, I quietly open the door to my room and tiptoe down the hall, careful not to make any moves that could wake anyone up. With each step I take, I replay past Thanksgiving preparation days in my mind, making sure that I have listed every ingredient I remember seeing on the counter as Mama bakes. The closer I get to the kitchen, the more I doubt that my plan to bake the pineapple sugar cake is going to work.

When I finally reach the kitchen, the confidence that led me to think that I could actually make the cake is gone.

"Safiri, I'm surprised to see you awake this early." Mama's voice startles me and pulls me out of my thoughts of pineapples and sugar.

I'm so startled that I let out a shrill scream. To my surprise, I look up to find Mama sitting up in a chair, mixing away at the batter in the big sunflower bowl she always uses to make her delicious pineapple cake. Mama, dressed in her favorite salmon colored robe, looks so beautiful. Looking as close to what I think a Thanksgiving miracle could ever look like, Mama waves her left hand towards me.

"Come help me with the cake since you're up!" she exclaims.

Stunned, but more than anything, relieved, I grab the green stool from the corner of the kitchen and pull it as close to Mama as I can.

"Mama, what are you doing? I thought you weren't cooking anything today?"

"Baby, I need to do something to make today feel right," she replies. "I've been making this cake for longer than I've been making Thanksgiving turkeys, that's for sure. The least I can do is give my family something sweet."

Now seems like the perfect time to go ahead and tell Mama about my big surprise. Besides, what a perfect way to let Mama know that we wouldn't be the only ones nibbling on the cake she is making.

Before I can decide whether or not to let go of the secret I have been keeping, Mama gets up and moves slowly toward the kitchen table where I see a medium-sized white box resting in the center. I guess I hadn't even noticed the box when I walked in the kitchen because I had been so focused on Mama.

She sits down and pushes the box toward where I'm standing.

"Open it," she directs, sharply.

Pulling the lid from the green and yellow striped box, I complement Mama on the yellow tissue covered in pineapples that she has used for wrapping paper.

I finally uncover the object at the bottom of the gift box. Peeking through all of the wrapping is what appears to be some sort of scrapbook. The yellow cover, of course, has a large pineapple glued to the front of it. I didn't expect anything less coming from Mama.

I am unsure what is inside of the book as I hold it in my hands. Looking at Mama, I peel back the wrapping tissue to uncover a yellow, ringed binder. Inside of the plastic cover is a sheet of Mama's lined, pineapple stationery with the words *Pineapple Sugar: Then Until Now* written into the center to the first page. Curiously,

I open the binder and immediately recognize a picture of a crayon-drawn turkey with a red gobbler scribbled all the way down to the bottom of the page. In the middle, right-hand side of the paper, I see what looks like one of my first attempts of my four-year-old hand at writing my name, as the *S* and *r* are proudly written backwards. I turn to the next page and see stick-figure pictures, each one seeming to tell its own story. Written on the back of each page is a date.

"What are these, Mama?" I ask, pointing to the dates.

"That's the day you drew the picture, baby."

As I flip through the pages, the pictures are gradually replaced with written words; the dates no longer written by Mama's hand, but by mine on the top of each page. I begin to realize that this work is not just from Thanksgivings past, but from individual moments of my life — those pineapple sugar moments that Mama made me record with those items from her purse I've always hated. She had saved them — every one.

The memories come rushing back to me as I turn the pages of my recorded life. I am nothing less than amazed by the woman I call Mama. She has taken everything I have ever written from one Thanksgiving to the next, and made probably the most beautiful gift I've ever received.

Mama breaks the long silence that has filled the room since I opened the green and yellow striped box.

"I figure the least I can do is come make this old cake today if I can't do anything else." She struggles up from the kitchen table and walks over to the kitchen counter. Mama says nothing about the precious gift that I hold in my hands. As she walks by, I see her eyes glisten with tears that don't fall. She begins to pour the last few ingredients into the mixing bowl to finish the pineapple sugar cake she had started.

The weight of the batter in Mama's frail arms leaves her nearly breathless as she tries to lift the cake batter from the kitchen counter to the oven. I rush from my stool to help her, carefully placing my hands under hers to keep the uncooked cake from hitting floor. I close the oven door as Mama returns to her seat at the table.

"Mama?" I call out softly.

Mama's elbow props on the kitchen table; her hand presses softly against her forehead.

I run to her and wrap my arms around her waist, laying my head against her chest. I listen to her heartbeat and close my eyes, trying to hold back my tears. Everything that I have ever thought to write on the pages of the binder that she has gifted to me is because of her. Every lesson that I have ever learned is because Mama has taught me how to see the good in things that could have easily broken me down. I hug Mama tightly because she is the greatest gift my life could have ever allowed me to have — even more than the binder of memories that I, now hold in my hands.

"What are you thankful for this year, Safiri?" Mama whispers.

"You, Mama."

The silence that comes after my reply is filled with so many unspoken words of love that both Mama and I begin to cry. We hold on to each other like we are holding on to our own lives. At least, that is what it feels like for me. Mama *is* my life, and without her, I don't know what I will do.

"Safiri, do you know how I get my Pineapple Sugar cakes just right every year?" Mama asks.

"No, ma'am," I reply.

"Every year since the day I knew you could hold a pencil, I have had you write about life and the pineapple sugar that comes with it. I have never needed a timer because I have you. When you sit down to write what you are thankful for, I know that you will always take a certain amount of time — a perfect amount of time. By the time were in second grade, your timing was perfect, and so were my pineapple sugar cakes! You are the reason my pineapple sugar cakes come out the way they do year after year. You, baby. It's all because of you."

Only Josephine Fields could turn something as simple as baking a cake into something so magical.

Squealing like a bird with no feathers, I ask Mama what seems to be a thousand and one more questions about the pineapple sugar cake, as well as the binder from the green and yellow striped box. She seems just as excited to answer my questions as I am about asking them.

In the middle of everything, the color seems to flush from Mama's face.

"I need to lay down, sugar." Mama's announcement brings me back to the reality that no matter how much fun Mama and I have together, and no matter how many new secrets we share, the fact still remains that she's sick.

I grab Mama's hand and lead her to her bedroom. Even though Daddy is sleeping on his side of the bed, I try not to wake him. I pull back the covers for Mama and help her get in a comfortable position.

"I will be alright, Safiri. I think I just need a little nap," Mama says softly.

Daddy wakes up with a confused look on his face. The way that he sits up and looks down at Mama lets both of us know that he had been too tired to even notice she had ever gotten up in the first place.

"Josephine, are you alright?" he asks Mama, wiping the sleep from his eyes.

"Don't worry. I will be okay, Vance. Safiri, take the cake out of the oven when it's ready, baby. Can you do that for me?"

"Yes, ma'am."

My heart nearly melts. Seeing Mama like this is causing me to think that my big Thanksgiving Day surprise may be too much for her to handle. Kissing Mama on the forehead, I cover her with the crimson blanket thrown across the foot of their bed. As I close their bedroom door behind me, once again, tears begin to fall; but this time, I can't do anything to stop them. I run straight to my room, lie across my bed, and cry so hard that I fall fast asleep.

I awake feeling better — at least better than I did after tucking Mama into her bed for a nap. Still, I can't dismiss the worry that I feel for her, so I decide to go check on Mama just to be sure that she really is okay, like she claims to be.

Half asleep, I push myself to get out of the bed. Suddenly, however, the strong smell of warm, sweet pineapples fills my room. I have grown to know and love that smell more and more each year, so there is no mistake in my mind that what I'm smelling is coming from the kitchen. For a brief moment, I am in pineapple sugar paradise, until suddenly; I remember what Mama had asked me to do.

"THE CAKE!" I scream. Somehow, I had managed to totally forget that Mama had left me in charge of the pineapple sugar cake that she had mixed earlier this morning. Making a mad dash down the hallway, down the stairs and into the kitchen, I grab the first towel I see. I slide toward the oven door, and yank it open, hoping that I have not spoiled Thanksgiving. But, I am too late. The smoke from the burnt cake takes over the kitchen as soon as I open the oven door.

Ruined! The smoke detector in the kitchen starts beeping uncontrollably. I stand there with the oven door wide open, holding the dishtowel that I had used to open it. Not knowing whether to get the cake out of the oven or try to turn off the smoke detector, I simply lose it. I cry so hard that I can barely breathe. The burnt cake however, is just a kick — start to everything I'm feeling right now, I admit. I turn off the oven and plop myself down in front of it. I close my eyes, and don't bother wiping my tears as the smoke alarm continues to sound. Once again, on the kitchen floor, I let myself cry about everything: life, Mama's sickness, and everything in between.

"Girl, you have got to dry those tears and pull it together. We've got a Thanksgiving dinner to get on the table!"

The familiar voice is startling but calming all at the same time.

"Aunt Annie-Lou!" I jump up off the floor and fling my arms around her neck.

"Well, I see we won't be having pineapple sugar cake this year," she laughs.

Taking one good look at the black mass that used to be a cake, together we burst into laughter. Aunt Annie-Lou always seems to know how to make me feel better about things. She has never been afraid to use the key that Mama and Daddy gave her to our house for emergencies, especially for non-emergency purposes.

"Honey, don't worry. The family went overboard on desserts this year anyway."

Before I could sigh in relief, Daddy and Mama dash into the kitchen, frightfully screaming my name. Seeing them come around the corner, I can tell that they are afraid, and have no idea what to expect. One thing is for sure, though: they certainly were not expecting to see my aunt standing there with me — especially not on Thanksgiving Day.

"Annie Lou! What in the world are you doing here?"

My Daddy looks a bit confused, seeing me, a burned cake, and my aunt in the middle of the kitchen. My Mama, still looking weak, holds on to his arm as he helps her into her chair at the kitchen table.

"Yeah, big sis. I'm glad to see you, but what are you doing here? I told you I'm not cooking this year, Loucie! Safiri, Vance, and I are going out to the have Thanksgiving lunch in about an hour or two."

"The heck you are!" Aunt Annie-Lou exclaims.

I love Aunt Annie-Lou. She never has a problem saying exactly what she feels, in the way she feels it needs to be said.

"Lady and gentleman," my aunt begins. "I think you better sit down. You're not going to believe what your daughter has done."

With that introduction, my aunt begins to tell my parents about the Thanksgiving dinner surprise that I have put together for our family. She starts the story with the night I called her about my idea, and she keeps on going from there. I can feel myself blushing as I stand there listening. I want to run, but I also want to stay and listen. This is a proud moment for me because I know that I am doing something special for Mama.

Mama bursts into laughter. Tears roll down her cheeks. She tries to speak to me, but each time she does, laughter takes over her. I look at Daddy who is simply staring at me now. As our eyes meet, he whispers, "I love you, little girl" to me as Mama finally pulls herself together to say something to me.

"Safiri, honey. How did you do this? I had no idea!" Mama's voice is stern but soft.

Just as I'm about to fess up about snooping around Mama's address book, the doorbell rings.

Thank God!

The doorbell becomes my excuse to leave the kitchen.

"I'll get it!" I exclaim, and I run to the front door.

I can hear Mama, Daddy, and Aunt Annie-Lou still talking about the newfound surprise as I run out of the kitchen. With the first ring of the doorbell, a sea of cousins, aunts, uncles, distant relatives, and family friends take over our kitchen where my parents and Aunt Annie-Lou are still talking about how I managed to pull off my secret Thanksgiving operation.

The kitchen soon reaches capacity, and the traffic spills into the dining room as one by one, folks come in making a fuss for somebody to "heat this up"; everybody hands over to Aunt Annie-Lou the dishes they have prepared and brought with them. Cakes and pies,

as well as sides and main dishes, overflow our counter-
tops and tables within a matter of minutes.

Mama looks so happy to be surrounded by family.
Her look of joy and love that I have known for my
entire life is all over her face. For a moment, it seems
as though everything is back to normal — like Mama's
sickness does not exist. What matters most right now is
that she is happy. And so am I.

*"Lord, grant peace to the family of our dear
sister Josephine Fields. May they learn to accept the things that cannot be changed. Lord,
give them strength to face everything day by
day...."*

My heart begins to beat in tempo with Uncle Jeffrie's
Thanksgiving blessing. His words touch my heart as we
stand holding hands in our family circle around the
dining room table. I *can't* change the fact that Mama
will not be here with me forever and my great-uncle's
prayer reminds me to cherish her one day at a time.

"Bless Safiri, God. Shine down on her and bring her serenity and confidence knowing that she, at such a young age, has brought joy to her family in a way that we will all remember..."

With those words, Mama opens her glossy eyes and looks straight at me. It has always been a rule in the Field's home to never open your eyes during the Thanksgiving prayer. Today, though, even Mama breaks that rule.

The prayer comes to an end, and like a choir singing in unison, we all say "Amen."

However, before we can dig in, Mama waves her hand in the air from left to right to get everyone's attention.

"Everyone, I have something I want to say," Mama announces.

Instantly, all eyes become focused on her as she speaks.

"Time is precious, I'm sure we have all learned that by now. I know I have. You may have noticed that we aren't having pineapple sugar cake today..."

"...and you may be burning to ask where exactly that cake is," interrupted Aunt Annie-Lou, laughing and looking straight at me.

Here we go.

"Watch it Annabel Louis," Mama snaps, grinning at her sister.

"As I was saying," Mama continues, "Safiri and I learned just today that even a perfectly mixed cake has to bake in the right amount of time — no more, no less."

Mama gives a quick smile and wink. Before I have the chance to feel embarrassed, she looks away and re-starts her speech.

"I have learned that lesson, especially, during these last few months. There is so much that I could say right now, but I just want to take the time to thank my daughter, Safiri Josephine Fields."

Everyone in the room looks at me, their smiles warm as the noonday sun. A high-pitched hand-clap breaks my gaze from Mama's. Before I can see who has of-fered the gesture, though, others follow. The next thing I know, they are all clapping — my entire family. The applause, cheering, and smiles seem to go on forever before the noise finally dies down.

"Sugar, you have made me so proud by putting to-gether this perfect day all by yourself," Mama begins again. "You just don't know what this has done for me; it makes me so proud to know that you already have what it takes inside of you to help you journey to becoming the woman that you were born to be. I love you, Safiri. You are more than I could have asked for."

There's not a dry eye in the room as I walk over to Mama and hug her as tightly as I can. As much as I am hers, Mama *is* my pineapple sugar. Our lives have treated us with bitterness, but the love we share is the sweetest thing I have ever known.

"Alright, let's eat!" Mama exclaims.

We break the family circle and everyone starts to cheer. The tearful mood of the room slowly breaks as we begin to fill our plates with every dish of our Thanksgiving potluck. There is something different this year; the room feels different, even though smiles and laughter take up the air of the room. Maybe it's just me. Maybe I am finally ready to admit that there's a chance this will be Mama's last Thanksgiving with us.

I feel proud that Operation Thanksgiving has come together. The sound of laughter and love has taken over the harsh quiet that has lived in our home since Mama got sick. The last bite has long since been taken, but the adults still sit around the table talking while the kids play together in the living room. The television is on, but no one is watching it. We are all enjoying each other's company here in Josephine's house — the way we do every Thanksgiving.

I look around the room at all of the smiling faces, only to quickly find that Mama is missing. She is usually the center of everything during Thanksgiving, so it's not difficult to notice that she isn't here.

I go from room to room to look for Mama, but I don't call her name. I don't want to bring any attention to the fact that she has slipped away from the family gathering. Even though I start to get worried that something is wrong, I continue to look throughout the house, checking all of the places that I know Mama goes when she wants peace and quiet.

It isn't long before I walk into my parents' bedroom and find Mama sitting in her big chair gazing out of the window.

I don't want to startle Mama, so I clear my throat just loud enough to bring her out of her deep though.

"Mama, are you alright?" I whisper slowly, and sit down beside her.

As she looks up at me, I wrap my arms around her neck and kiss her on the cheek.

"Hi, Safiri. I'm fine. I just need to rest for a minute. You didn't have to come and find me, baby."

For someone who has always loved to be around her family during the Thanksgiving holiday, seeing Mama here, alone in her room, saddens me. In all of this time since Mama has been fighting for her life, we have always talked about me — about the things she wants me to keep doing despite her sickness. In the last few days, Mama has given me so many opportunities to talk to her and ask her questions that I have always wanted to know the answers to, and she has responded with so much truth and understanding. But I realize that not one time have I asked her about her feelings. Not once have I given her the chance to tell me about what she is feeling. I have brought all of our family members here to share this Thanksgiving with us, but not one time have I invited Mama to share her true feelings with me about what she is going through.

I begin to feel selfish — as if I am the reason Mama is here in this room by herself while the rest of us are laughing and smiling in the home that she has always opened up to everyone. I do my best to untangle the possibilities of what Mama is feeling because I suddenly feel like it is my job to fix it. I want to be here for her the way that she is always there for me. I want to ask the right questions and say the right things. Whatever it takes to make her know that she isn't alone.

"Mama, are you scared?"

The long pause that comes before Mama's response is like a foreign language to me. She is usually so sure of her answers to me, as if she magically knows what I am going to say before I even say it. Her silence now, though, seems to answer me before she even opens her mouth.

"I don't know, Safiri," she replies. "I really don't know."

I take the time to look Mama from head to toe. Her body looks frail — a long way away from what I've always known her to be. Her eyes still glow, though. Somehow, those big brown eyes let me know that even though Mama has always been a fighter, I am witnessing the most important battle that she will ever fight.

She lets out a soft chuckle and shifts the weight of her body to the chair's armrest. "I'll be able to stay close to the ones I love no matter how far apart they are from one another. That's a plus!" she laughs. "Who knows? If I'm really lucky, I may even be able to check in on everybody at the same time!"

Mama's chuckle turns into laughter. But her laugh is one I've never heard before. It is deep and slow. She looks upward toward the ceiling, and just as quickly, squeezes her eyes shut tightly. I watch as her laughter suddenly changes into a low-pitched sob. Right in front of me, my strong and mighty Mama, who has overcome everything that she has ever faced, seems to be bowing down to fear and sadness. The reality is that she has every right to be afraid. Who wouldn't be scared to die?

I try to put myself in Mama's shoes. I search for the right words to say to her but instead, decide to challenge Mama in a way that I never have. No matter how hard it may seem, I figure if Mama could push me to find the pineapple sugar in everything I have ever been through in my life, the least I can do is be the one to help her do the same when it counts the most.

I walk over to Mama's nightstand junk drawer to rally a pen and a piece of the stationery paper that she uses to write her *thinking of you* notes to most of the people now sitting around our dining room table.

"Mama?"

Lifting her eyes from the tears that have fallen into her hands, she looks into the sunlight that shines through the bedroom window.

"What is it, baby?"

I take a deep breath and lay the pen and paper in front of Mama and walk towards the door.

"Mama, what's your pineapple sugar story this year?"

As I turn the doorknob to leave, I see Mama watching me, nearly in disbelief. Making sure that she understands what she is supposed to do, I take a page out of her own book and charge her to do something that she has been requiring me to do for about the last eight Thanksgivings:

"Josephine Fields, tell me your story, and then give me the pineapple sugar."

When the sirens and the red lights outside of my bedroom window wake me up, I look at the clock and see that it is only 3:42 a.m. My heart nearly stops because I already know; there is no confusion — not even a moment of wondering — if Mama is the reason for all of the commotion outside.

"Mama!" I yell.

I run downstairs just in time to see the paramedics roll Mama into the back of the ambulance with Daddy grasping her hand.

"Daddy! Mama!"

Those are the words that my mouth is supposed to say, but I quickly realize that nothing — not one sound, is coming out of it. My chest begins to hurt and I gasp for air. I can't seem to catch my breath. My head begins to hurt and everything I see begins to spin. My knees begin to weaken and my flailing arms search for something to grab onto, but there is nothing that can keep me from going down. My knees give out first, and then my legs. My arms become still and hang downward.

Before I can hit the ground, Aunt Annie-Lou grabs me at my shoulders and pulls me towards her chest. The weight and downward momentum of my limp body taking such a fall is too much for her to keep upright. I feel us both touch the ground — my aunt struggling to place herself underneath me to protect me from getting hurt. The last things I remember are the faces of neighbors who have come outside amidst all the ruckus of the ambulance's lights and sirens. They are rushing toward us, calling my name with their arms stretched out toward my aunt and me.

I feel us fall, but their hands catch us. I bury my head into Aunt Annie-Lou's chest, squeeze my eyes shut and just cry.

chapter 8:

A FIT CELEBRATION

Mama was brought to this hospital seven days ago. All of the family members who traveled long distances to be here for Thanksgiving dinner have gone. For seven days, Mama has been hooked up to breathing machines and heart monitors; needles have pierced her arms, drawing blood and giving her what her body cannot provide. Aunt Annie-Lou is staying with me while Daddy spends most nights at the hospital with Mama. There has never in my life been such a time when I could not shake the feeling that something is terribly wrong – that something bad is going to happen. The feeling is so strong that I can almost touch it.

After days of begging Aunt Annie-Lou to take me to see Mama, she finally does.

"Your Mama wouldn't want me to let you see her like this," she protested.

I know — we all know — that Mama wouldn't want me to see her at such a low point. But the truth is, she hasn't gotten any better.

"Aunt Annie-Lou. I need to see my Mama!"

My persistence pays off because I'm standing here in hospital room 216.

It's just like Mama to try and sit up to give me the biggest smile that she can.

"Hi, sugar," she whispers, as if we are sitting at home in the living room.

To look at Mama, however, I know that she is far from well. In fact, the show that she puts on for me makes everything about her stay in this hospital seem worse than I believed it to be before Aunt Annie-Lou agreed to let me see her. Her shoulders shrug as she tries to sit up to greet me. Her entire body seems hunched over like it's too painful to unfold itself. Her arms look frail as she reaches out to hug me. As I feel her try not to rest the weight of her body around my shoulders, Mama's hug is nothing more than a gentle touch. Her smile, however, is untouched: it's the only part of Mama that seems to be unharmed by the sickness that has taken over her body.

"Mama, are you okay?" I ask softly.

She lets out a deep sigh. "I am okay, Safiri."

Both of us look each other up and down before our eyes come together. To look at her, I know she isn't telling me the truth. Mama looks away, as if she knows exactly what I am thinking.

After that, Mama and I sit together in silence. I rest my head on the hospital bed rail as I hold Mama's hand. Every now and then, Mama asks me a question about school and I pretend, as best as I can, that whatever I have to say matters at all.

We fall off to sleep somewhere in between Family Feud and the five o'clock news.

"Well, would you look at that!" Aunt Annie-Lou's laughter brings Mama and me out of our naptime.

"Hey, sis. It's good to see you. Thank you for bringing my baby to me," Mama says.

"Honey, are you kidding me? You think *your* daughter would have it any other way?"

We all laugh as best as we can. I can see Mama's eyes turn a little red; it's easy to see that she wants to cry, but she doesn't. Not with me standing there looking at her, at least.

When it is time to go, I give Mama a big hug. "I love you, mama. You are the best mama in the world."

"I love too, sugar. You make me so proud."

As Aunt Annie-Lou and I leave the hospital, there is nothing I can do to keep back the tears that have been waiting to fall.

I am not exactly sure how to explain it, but some tiny voice inside of my head seems to be getting louder and louder, and it's wearing me down. The noise makes my heart strings vibrate like the strings of Daddy's guitar. It plays like a song that only I can hear. The message is not a melody, though. This tiny voice sings to me that Mama's time here with us will be ending very soon.

Mama once told me that when we are facing death, we have two choices:

"Safiri, we can either run away from it in fear, knowing that at some point, it is going to catch up with us anyway, or we can look it straight in the eyes, welcome its challenge, and peacefully surrender to it," she explained. "Only those of us who are at peace with ourselves, our lives, and our loved ones can do the latter."

As much as dying is Mama's journey, it has come to be mine as well. Before, I wasn't at peace with anything. Hearing that your Mama is leaving and there is nothing that you can do about is not for the faint of heart. Who at school can you talk to about it? Who can possibly understand how one minute you are fine, and the next, you're crying and screaming on the kitchen floor feeling helpless?

I can honestly say that I have been learning how to let Mama go. There is an undying bond between Mama and me that is woven together like fabric. Mama knows this — she was the first to know, of course. It may sound silly, but I don't think she will let go of her life, or the life that she has been forced to have through her horrible sickness, until I am ready to let her go. It is almost like Josephine Fields has made a deal with God, a bargain that is letting her hang on by the short thread of life she has left inside of her body, until I make peace with everything. Simply put, Mama isn't going to die until she knows that I will be alright.

As much as I want Mama here with me, I know that keeping her here the way she is now is pretty selfish. My Mama will never be the same. Her body will never get as strong as it once was. She will never be able to stand in the kitchen and cook all night as she once did, and she won't ever be able to come and go the way that she always has been known to do. If she lives, for the rest of her life, she will always have to be cared for — never again able to do anything for herself. I know my Mama enough to know that for her, that's not living. Mama isn't just someone who can exist: she has to be larger than life. So, simply lying in a bed, barely able to muster enough strength to walk, would do more to her than this sickness ever could — it would kill her soul.

The thoughtful goodness Mama has put into the world makes it easy for me to know exactly what I need to do for her as she lies in the hospital bed of room 216. I want Mama to know that I *can* give thanks for life's pineapple sugar moments no matter how difficult the lesson. I need her to believe in my strength to follow through on everything she has ever taught me about life.

Being twelve, I don't have much to give my Mama. There is no magical cure to what has taken over her body. Whatever is going to happen, I can't change. But I need to show Mama that I will be okay — that it is alright for her to stop suffering.

The only help I can offer Mama is a simple gift, but it's mine — one that Mama helped me to discover. I will write Mama an ending to her story; the ending

129

that she deserves. It will be one of love and of peace. The idea comes so incredibly quickly that I'm scared I will lose it. There's no time to get to my notebook. I look on the counter for paper and a pen. Right where I am, in the middle of the kitchen floor, I begin to write the best story I've ever written. I never thought that my most important story would be written for Mama.

The lights twinkled as Queen Josephine stood to take her throne. All the people in Pineapple Sugarville loved her and were happy to welcome her to her new home. Queen Josephine was kind and loving, and brought with her all of the love from the world she had come from. Unsure of why the citizens of Pineapple Sugarville had chosen her as their queen when she had only just arrived, Queen Josephine sat on her throne trying to remember everything she had ever done that could be seen as good. Suddenly, a crystal ball appeared beside her. Inside the ball, she saw her memories — memories of people she had loved who had sent her on her mystical journey to Pineapple Sugarville. Within this magic crystal, she saw how every good thing she had ever done for anyone had been transformed

into the magic that moved her higher and higher, until she arrived in the new land where she ruled as Queen. Even though she missed her old friends and family, she looked around Pineapple Sugarville and saw that there was work to be done.

In her crystal ball, Queen Josephine was proud to see that Princess Safiri was busy at work, carrying out all of the work that her mother, Queen Josephine, had taught her to do before she had left for Pineapple Sugarville. All of the love from Queen Josephine lived on in Princess Safiri, who finally learned to find the good in everything, even those things that seemed as if there was no good in them to be found…

Mama can no longer sit up. As I read my story to her, she slowly pats the bed rail with her hand. I sit next to her, careful not to disturb the machines and tubes that are giving her life right now. I don't hesitate to take advantage of the chance to be as close to Mama as possible.

"I love you, Sugar. Thank you for being so thoughtful. You are more than I could have ever asked for in a daughter."

Mama no longer sounds like Josephine. Her voice is now soft — just above a whisper. I can tell talking is a painful chore. Still that doesn't stop her from letting me know that she appreciates what I've done.

"I love you, too, Mama."

I lay my head next to hers. We rest in silence long enough for me to see the five o'clock news come on and Mama drift off to sleep.

chapter 9:
WHEN IT'S ALL SAID AND DONE

I lie in bed, completely still. The clock says that it is 1:36 a.m. and still, I cannot sleep. Daddy is staying with Mama at the hospital tonight, something he has been doing a lot of lately. The house is quiet without my parents here. Mama has been on my mind since we got home from the hospital. I have never seen her this way — sick and unable to do things on her own. Staring at the open door, I can't help but keep Mama on my mind imagining her in the hospital room connected to so many machines. Lying in my bed, I let the weight of the covers fall heavy over my arms as I imagine how closed in and tied down Mama must feel in her hospital bed.

Suddenly, the phone rings. In the space between my bedroom door and the floor, I see the lights come on downstairs. A sinking feeling takes over my stomach and I sit straight up in my bed.

I hear my aunt's voice as she answers the phone, but I can't hear exactly what she is saying. I know that something is wrong. I can feel it. No one ever calls this late. The only thing that anyone would call about at such an hour is Mama.

As the sound of my aunt's footsteps get closer, they get slower and slower. I clench the covers of my bed, and wait.

"Safiri?" Aunt Annie-Lou stands in the doorway of my room. She jumps back a bit, startled to see me already sitting up, waiting on her.

"Safiri, put some clothes on. It is time to go to the hospital." Aunt Annie-Lou walks into my room without saying a word. I slowly get out of bed knowing that the end is here.

Looking at Aunt Annie-Lou on the drive to the hospital, I can tell she has been crying.

"Aunt Annie-Lou, did Mama die?"

By the way she looks at me, I can tell that my question is unexpected. One thing that I know about my aunt, however, is that no matter what, just like her sister, she will tell me the truth.

"No sweetie, she is still hanging on for us," she replies.

I knew that this moment would come eventually — the one where we have to say goodbye to Mama, but it still hits me pretty hard. I have worked so hard to let Mama go…to make her see I will be all right. But will I really be? Can I really survive without my Mama? Am I really strong enough to keep living after she dies?

I know the answers to my own questions. Mama has shown us all how to look both the good and the bad in the face and not flinch. I have to do whatever I can to stop being scared and realize that I am made from the same stuff as Mama: strength, determination, and love. If she can face death, I can face anything, including letting her go.

The hospital room is quiet. An awkward silence is only interrupted by the sound of the machines keeping Mama alive. Daddy rests on his knees with his head propped against the bottom of Mama's feet. His head is down and his eyes are closed. Over him stands a man dressed in a black suit with a white collar. The badge that hangs from his shirt pocket says "clergy".

I walk towards Daddy and wrap my arm around his shoulder. He looks up at me with tears clouding his eyes.

"Hello, honey," he whispers to me as he leans in to give me a hug.

Immediately, I feel selfish. All of this time, I had been worried about my own struggle in losing Mama. I had never stopped to think about the fact that Daddy is losing someone he has known longer than I have even existed.

Aunt Annie-Lou comes and stands beside me and Daddy. She tends to Mama — brushing back the loose hairs that have fallen into Mama's eyes.

Beep...beep...beep...

The machine on Mama's left side begins to hum slower and slower.

"Are you sure you want your child in here for this?" asks the man with the clergy badge.

I don't want anyone making this decision for me. Right now, Mama is simply asleep — that's how I am choosing to remember her.

Not giving anyone a chance to push me out of hospital room 216, I lean over and kiss Mama on the cheek.

"I love you, Mama. Thank you for all of your pineapple sugar."

As I walk out of the room, I hear the machine make one final beep that doesn't stop.

Mama is gone.

chapter 10:

PINEAPPLE SUGAR

With all of the pressure I am feeling in the days leading up to Mama's funeral service, all I want to do is lock myself inside of my room and imagine that all of this is just a bad dream.

I close my eyes and dream that my Mama is right downstairs where she has always been. When I open my eyes though, Mama is nowhere around.

Since Mama died, Daddy hasn't said much, but neither have I. Since that morning, Aunt Annie-Lou has been staying with us, and if it wasn't for her, I doubt either one of us would have eaten anything. She's been wonderful to have around. Tonight, she is taking some time to take care of things around her own house, though.

"I've got to let the roaches know I still live there before they move in," she joked.

A firm knock sounds at my door and without a second thought, I know it's my aunt.

She must have decided to come back early to make sure we are okay.

"Come in," I reply, as I wait for my aunt to peek her head through my doorway.

I am more than surprised as Daddy, not Aunt Annie-Lou, enters my room. He looks tired and worn. Clearing his throat, he does not even try to hide his pain. His voice is shaky.

"Safiri, honey, write something to say at the service. Your Mama would have wanted that."

Before I can even open my mouth to protest, he turns and leaves the room.

What can I possibly say at my own Mama's funeral? What can I say that would mean something to everyone and make Mama proud at the same time?

Speaking at Mama's funeral is just something that I don't want to do. Living through everything I've been through over the last several days is enough for me. I'm not sure what Daddy is thinking, but all I plan to do for Mama's service is get through it.

"Daddy!" I call out. But he does not answer.

I take my time going downstairs to find Daddy. No matter what I have to do, I am determined to get out of the speaking role he's decided to give me. I stop quickly in my tracks when I get to the kitchen and find Daddy sitting in Mama's chair at the table. Holding his guitar, he doesn't even notice me as I walk in and stand behind him. It crosses my mind not to bother him; he seems captivated by his own melody, his fingers strumming his guitar, playing a tune familiar to this house. I watch and listen to Daddy play *Josephine* to a tempo that doesn't quite seem to fit the song — it's rhythm drags the melody along as he hums the notes that he's always sung to Mama.

"Daddy?"

Although I know he hears me calling him, Daddy still does not respond — at least not with words. I walk toward him only to see his glossy eyes are red from crying. Still, Daddy does not stop plucking the strings of his guitar. As he comes to the end of the melody, he finally sings the familiar words:

> "*...pineapple sugar is always within my reach...*"

As Daddy plays the last chord of *Josephine,* he turns and lifts his head just enough to catch my glance.

"Hi, Safiri."

Daddy's voice drifts into the air as he speaks. Even though he is sitting right in front of me, it seems as if his mind is thousands of miles away.

I decide to put my protest about speaking at Mama's funeral on hold. Determined to lift Daddy's spirits, I search for something that will not only make Daddy smile, but me as well.

Suddenly, an idea hits me. I can barely keep myself under control as I run out of the kitchen as fast as I can.

"I'll be right back, Daddy!" I exclaim from the hallway that leads from the kitchen to my room.

I rush to my nightstand and grab the ringed binder Mama had given me the day I burned her Thanksgiving pineapple sugar cake. Careful not to drop it, I hold it close to my chest as I run back to the kitchen where Daddy, still sitting in Mama's chair, has rested his guitar on the table.

"You know," he begins. "I've learned that any time you get *really* excited about something, I need to prepare myself for just about anything."

Watching me with a suspicious eye, Daddy gives me his full attention — the same way Mama always did whenever I had a big idea.

I hand him the scrapbook and begin telling him about the time I had spent with Mama each year as she baked. I go on, narrating the pictures from each year.

Daddy especially enjoys the part where I tell him about how Mama told me that she used me each year to make sure that her pineapple sugar cakes came out just right.

"I had no idea!" he says, not taking his eyes off the pages of the binder in his hands.

Daddy's tear-stained eyes seem to light up as he slowly flips through each page, as if he is reliving each year represented by my writing.

I feel like this is a good time to make my case against having to speak at Mama's funeral. One more page of the scrapbook, and Daddy will be crying, again.

"Daddy, you know how you said I had to say something at Mama's memorial service?"

Daddy doesn't look up, but from the way he turns his head slightly toward me, I know he is listening. Just when I am about to go through with my original plan of canceling my speech for Mama's funeral, I see his eyes well up with tears. I glance downward at the page where he has stopped. As he traces his finger against the page where Mama's handwriting is, I understand why he is crying.

"Honey, have you seen this?"

Daddy points to a page near the back of the binder. I honestly had not taken time to look through every page when Mama gave it to me the morning that I burned her pineapple sugar cake. Curiously, I look over his shoulder to the place where his fingers trace. We lock our eyes in synch on the last page of the binder, where a message has been written in handwriting that is unmistakably not mine — handwriting that I have come to know over the years from surprise love notes in my lunch box, signed report cards, and birthday cards.

"Is that what I think it is, Daddy?"

He shakes his head to respond.

"That woman is unbelievable. That's my girl."

As Daddy smiles, I reread the page that, to my surprise, holds the recipe to Mama's famous pineapple sugar cake. It's written on a small piece of worn paper stained in flour and pineapple filling. Underneath the recipe, is a note:

> *Safiri,*
>
> *Keep living. Keep writing. Keep finding the pineapple sugar.*
>
> *Love,*
> *Mama*

"Safiri, I just got the craziest idea."

Hearing Daddy talk about crazy ideas is new; it's strangely exciting, especially during a time like this. He definitely has my attention. Whatever can keep Daddy from being totally down from Mama's death has my vote.

"Make the cake," he says calmly.

"What do you mean make the cake, Daddy?"

Daddy didn't take his eyes off of Mama's handwritten note and the cake recipe.

"For the funeral, Safiri...that's what you are going to do. Forget a long speech. You are going to make your Mama's pineapple sugar cake — lots and lots of it."

Oh my God. Daddy's lost his mind.

I must be wearing my thoughts on my face like I always do, because he keeps talking.

"Hear me out, honey," he says, nearly pleading. "Your Mama was in no way an ordinary woman and you know that."

I can at least nod in agreement with this. Nothing that had anything to do with Mama was simple or ordinary. Every moment that centered around Mama had always been extraordinary and memorable.

"Safiri, your Mama will always be a big part of my life. I have known her forever, and something inside of me is telling me that this is something she would want you to do."

"Daddy! The last time I had anything to do with making the pineapple sugar cake, it burned!" I yelled. "Now, you want me to make the whole thing? I can't!"

I glance around the room, as if my decision will be helped along by something in our kitchen. The only thing that catches my eye, though, is Daddy's guitar that he'd been playing earlier.

Wait a minute.

I have an idea that goes right along with Daddy's crazy plan. I almost don't believe I'm going to go along with all of this, but if there's anyone right now that I am willing to do anything for, it's my daddy.

"I will do it under one condition, Daddy."

Daddy perks up to the point that I almost think he will come straight out of his chair, like a rocket.

"What's that, baby girl?"

"I will make the cake for the funeral if you play *Josephine* while everyone eats it!"

Even though my suggestion isn't as weird as Daddy's idea to have cake at Mama's funeral, he laughs heartily, as if I've just asked him to skate to the moon.

Daddy lets out a long exhale and picks up his guitar as he turns to face me.

"Sing it at the service?" he asks.

"Yep. At the service," I reply. I try to keep a straight, serious face so that Daddy knows that it's all or nothing — either he sings, or I don't make the cake.

He pauses for a brief moment and then extends his hand.

"Young lady, you've got yourself a deal. But first, I think there is something you should see. This time, *I'll* be right back."

For a moment, Daddy's eyes light up like they would when Mama was around. So whatever it is that has him so excited has to be something extremely special.

When Daddy comes back to the kitchen, he holds his hands behind his back so that I cannot see them.

"Close your eyes."

Like a little kid at Christmas, I shut my eyes so tight it nearly hurts. Before I have time to complain, Daddy gives his next command.

"Okay...open 'em!"

When I open my eyes, I see an old, cardboard-covered book with the word "journal" inscribed in gold on the bottom right hand corner.

There is something familiar about what's in front of me, but my memory draws a blank. I feel like I should know this — just like the binder Mama gave me on Thanksgiving morning.

"Look at it, honey. Just open it."

The green, yellow, and white cover that is tattered and torn seems at home sitting on the table where Daddy has placed it. I stare at it for a second, because strangely, there is something that lets me know I've seen this journal before.

Wait a minute...there's no way.

"Mama!" I scream. I quickly realize that I am looking at the journal that I had bought at my school store for Mama, right after Gran died. I had never known whether she had kept it, or even used it, for that matter. But looking at its worn cover, I feel sure that Mama must have had plenty to write about in it.

"After you gave this to your Mama, she wrote in this thing every night. Safiri, she would write and cry, and then write some more until one day, the crying just stopped. That's how I knew your Mama was going to be all right. That's also how I knew that you were the most special and thoughtful little girl in the world."

I am not sure if Daddy's goal is to make me cry or make me love him even more than I already do. Whichever one he has planned though, he succeeds at both.

"Daddy?"

"Yes, baby?" he replies.

"Do you want to help me make the cake?"

Daddy smiles and stands to give me a hug.

"Your Mama and I are so blessed to have you as a daughter, Safiri."

I'm surprised to hear Daddy speak of Mama as if she is still here. But I am glad about it. Even though Mama is gone, she will always be here, not just in our hearts, but in everything that we do to show each other love — especially right now as we get ready to make the pineapple sugar cake that she never got to finish on Thanksgiving.

"Let me help you get that flour off of the shelf, Safiri. Your Mama always complains about how heavy that jar is."

I mix, pour, and bake as Daddy plays his guitar. We share stories about Mama and laugh so much that no one in their right mind would probably ever believe that we are getting ready to go to a funeral.

After we put the first cake in the oven, Daddy holds his hand up for me to give him a high-five. All of a sudden, a strange look comes over his face. He jumps back from the oven.

"Oh shoot! We've got to call Reverend Bingham to make sure that it's okay to do this! I'll be right back!"

Daddy mutters under his breath as he walks out the kitchen, but I can't make out what he's saying. I start to think about it, and he's right — besides communion bread, no food has ever entered the sanctuary in my lifetime.

The joy that filled the kitchen just moments ago turns into disappointment. All of the happiness that Daddy seemed to get from our quest to make pineapple sugar cakes for Mama's funeral is about to tank. I'm sure of it.

All of a sudden, Daddy runs back into the kitchen and slides across the floor in his socks.

"Reverend Bingham gave us the green light! He even offered to rally his ushers to help us pass it out!"

"YEEEESSSSS!!!"

I can't believe it. In the midst of everything going wrong, this — this pineapple sugar cake plan is going right. Suddenly, a warm feeling surrounds me and I just know — I know Mama's hands are guiding every move that Daddy and I are making in the kitchen this evening. It's her spirit of love that makes Daddy pick up his old guitar and play with excitement like he's in concert at Carnegie Hall as we celebrate.

"Alright, you ready, Safiri?" Daddy asks as he grabs a stack of mixing bowls from underneath the cabinet.

"Ready, Daddy."

We bake, and bake, and bake until we've made twelve pineapple sugar cakes.

"One for every year you've been here, girl!" Daddy decides.

Tonight, I am beginning to learn that love really never stops; it just changes forms when it has to. So while Mama can't be here with us, everything she taught Daddy and me is here in this kitchen right now.

Not one of the twelve cakes burns. Not a single one.

chapter 11:
THE DAY

The smell of homemade breakfast fills my room and wakes me up. It has been so long since I've had Mama's homemade breakfast that my stomach immediately begins to rattle and growl for its first meal of the day. I jump straight up with one thought on my mind – a thought so exciting that I blurt it out, "Mama!"

However, as I reach for the doorknob my excitement vanishes. I realize that there is no way that Mama could be in the kitchen this morning. Today is the day that we say goodbye to her, and Aunt Annie-Lou had promised to come over this morning to help get me ready for the funeral service.

I am thankful to have Aunt Annie-Lou. She has always been there for me no matter what. I have never had to ask her for help; she never gives me that opportunity. When she sees the need, she offers it freely. She knew I would need her here this morning before I ever did.

I am nervous about my part on the funeral program. Aside from baking the pineapple sugar cakes, I spent so much time last night planning what I could possibly say about Mama, that all of my words now seem to be running together. Thankful for my midnight decision to write down my speech, I go to my desk to read through it one more time.

"No turning back now," I coach myself as I tuck the speech into the black purse I picked out last night to go with the same color dress I'm going to wear to Mama's service. As sad as today is going to be, I'm thankful that I've been to a few funerals before — enough to know that black is the color that you're supposed to wear.

Walking downstairs to greet Aunt Annie-Lou, I begin to wonder how Daddy is doing this morning. After we baked cakes, he got busy perfecting his pineapple sugar song. Even after I went to my room for bed, he was still going. I kept my door open to listen. It was almost as if Daddy was singing me a bedtime lullaby. The last thing I remember before drifting off to sleep was Daddy playing those familiar chords to *Josephine* on his guitar.

"Good morning, Aunt Annie-Lou."

My aunt turns around from the stove and gives me a big smile. I never noticed how much she looks like Mama when she smiles — not until today.

"Good morning, Safiri." Come get something to eat, baby. I made you some breakfast."

Walking towards my chair at the kitchen table, I notice that Aunt Annie-Lou has made a pot of coffee, but only half is left. This lets me know that Daddy is awake because my aunt doesn't drink coffee but my dad never starts the morning without it.

"Should I wait for Daddy?"

"No, baby. Your Daddy has already eaten. He's in his room getting ready now. Come on and eat with me. Besides, I have a surprise for you," she replies.

A surprise? On a day like this? My mind is curious. With a surprise from my aunt on a day like this, I am unsure of what to expect.

Aunt Annie-Lou sits my plate on the table.

"Go ahead and eat. I'll be right back."

Before I can fix my mind to wonder about the mystery of her surprise, my aunt returns with a yellow and white gift box with a huge, forest green bow. It looked just like something Mama would have approved.

"Is this for me, Aunt Annie-Lou?" I asked.

"Well, it sure isn't for me, honey! Open it!"

I slowly untie the bow, and remove the top of the box. Peeking out from underneath all of the gift-wrap tissue paper is a beautiful, cream-colored dress with yellow trim. The matching purse is extra special. It's patent leather with tiny pineapples that line the inside.

"I think this may be better than that black dress I know you're planning on wearing. Girl, you know that thing is probably too short. You haven't worn it in six months!"

Yep. She's right! I didn't even bother trying it on.

"Aunt Annie-Lou, it's beautiful!" I exclaim. I take the dress from her and put it against my chest to see how it looks against my skin.

"Girl, that looks wonderful on you!" she compliments. "But I can't take the credit. It's not from me."

"Well, who is it from if it's not from you?" I ask, confused.

"It looks like there's a card on the inside of that box, Safiri. You may as well read it," she replies sarcastically.

A little, pink card is taped beneath the white tissue that had held the dress. The pink stands out, but adds a different splash of color that makes the gift even more exciting than it already is. The note's glittery ink and large print makes it easy to read:

Safiri,
Whenever I'm feeling down, I always wear
something that's the opposite color of what
I'm feeling. I'm so sorry about your mom. I
hope this dress makes you feel a little better
today.

Your friend,
Michele

P.S :I know we haven't talked in a while and
I'm really sorry about that because I miss you.

"This is from *Michele?*" I asked in disbelief.

"Yep. Her mom called yesterday morning asking what size you wear. She said that Michele wouldn't let her rest until she went and got that dress. They'll both be there today, so you can thank them yourself."

"But...we.."

"Now sit down here and finish your breakfast," Aunt Annie-Lou interrupted sternly. "Today is going to be a long day."

I couldn't agree with her more.

It's a little funny to me that people use limousines to get to funerals. The only other times I have ever seen them are when movie stars arrive at the big award shows that come on television. When their drivers open their car doors, the camera people yell the stars' names hoping that they will turn around and pose for a good picture.

Unlike those celebrities, I have never been in a limousine in my entire life, and the first time I get the chance is to say goodbye to Mama, today. There will be no flashing cameras and no one calling my name. I am no celebrity. I am just a girl whose mother died.

The limousine driver seems to take the long route as he drives Daddy, Aunt Annie-Lou, and me to Trinity Zion Baptist Church. Pulling into the church's parking lot, the car makes two quick turns around the cars already parked. He suddenly stops the car and Daddy lets down the tinted window just in time to see the driver examine the cars on either side of our path. Nodding his head, he gets back into the limousine.

"Looks like it's a full house in there," he says, turning to look at us over his right shoulder. "There's nowhere else to park, so folks have started parking in the aisles of the lot! I wasn't sure if we would fit through, but we've got just enough room to get you front door service."

Daddy sits back in his seat and smiles as the limousine makes its way to the front doors of the church.

"I wouldn't expect anything different. My Josephine always could draw a crowd." Daddy's voice drifts out of the window as he lets it back up.

As the limousine driver opens our car door, Daddy shakes his hand and thanks him. He reaches back for my hand as I follow behind him. Aunt Annie-Lou uses her fingers to comb my curls that are out of place. I do my best to smooth the wrinkles that have made their way to the back of my dress.

"Don't worry about those, honey. You're going to be sitting down again soon and those wrinkles will be right back again. You look absolutely beautiful. I'm so proud of you."

Aunt Annie-Lou's eyes fill with tears as she hugs me and pulls a handkerchief from her purse.

"Go on with your Daddy, baby. I'm right here behind you every step of the way."

Turning from my Aunt, I squeeze Daddy's hand and look up at him. He holds his gaze forward toward the two church ushers who come and greet us. Reverend Bingham is standing in front of the closed sanctuary doors, waiting for us.

"Bless you all," he says shaking Daddy's hand. "Are we ready?"

Daddy looks down at me as if he's waiting on me to answer Reverend Bingham.

"I'm ready," I say softly.

The doors of the church open, and the organist plays a hymn as the congregation sings:

> *When we all get to heaven,*
> *What a day of rejoicing that will be!*
> *When we all see Jesus,*
> *We'll sing and shout the victory!*

Reverend Bingham leads us down the center aisle of the church as the congregation stands and faces us on either side. The smell of fresh flowers fills the church as we walk toward the white and yellow roses that surround the silver box that holds Mama's remains. The closed casket is a beautiful tribute to Mama; a decision that Daddy and I made so that everyone would remember her the way she was before the sickness took over.

As we sit in the front church pew, an usher hands us the colorful funeral programs that Aunt Annie-Lou, Daddy and I worked together to arrange. The entire first page is covered with a collage of pictures of Mama with different family and friends. Near the bottom of the page is the special picture that she took with Maisy, Kimberly, Eileen the day Mama gave me my new phone. The second page of pictures, however, looks more like a family photo album than anything. Pictures of Mama with Daddy when they were younger, all of us at the hospital when I was born, and family Christmas photos taken every year, fill the page.

Reverend Bingham begins the program with prayer and the choir stands to sing another song. A few friends and family members are then given a chance to line up and share special stories that honor Mama's memory.

The program moves along as it is printed, and we come to the place that reads, "*Special Reflections by Vance and Safiri Fields.*" Reverend Bingham calls my name and tells the congregation that Daddy and I will be doing something "a little bit untraditional" for a funeral service, but jokes that it is sure to be "in good taste."

I take a deep breath and reach for the speech I have thankfully written down and put in my purse last night.

The second I reach down, I realize my mistake.

My purse!

I had planned on wearing the black dress with the black purse. When Aunt Annie-Lou gave me my new outfit this morning, I was so excited that I forgot to move my speech to my new purse!

My palms start to sweat, and I begin to panic. What was I going to do without my speech? What could I possibly say that would make sense? I was already bringing cake to a funeral, so folks would already think I had gone off the deep end because of Mama's death. Now, I will be stumbling over words too!

For a moment, I am paralyzed. The congregation is waiting patiently for me to get up from my seat. My heart is beating faster and faster with every passing moment.

I will just tell Daddy that I don't want to do it anymore. He'll understand.

At first, this seems like the best idea. Then, I begin to think about Mama and remember how strong she taught me to be for moments just like this and realize that there's a chance that if I don't get up to say my speech, I will probably regret it for the rest of my life.

I can do this.

Everyone's eyes are on *my* every move since my name is on the service's program. It's too late to turn back now. Daddy gives me an approving head nod, which is just the push I need to rebuild the courage to do what we had planned the evening before.

I walk towards the podium that the ushers have set for me. With one glance at the congregation, I clear my throat, close my eyes, and breathe my speech out:

"Anyone who knows Mama knows about her famous pineapple sugar cake. This year at Thanksgiving, we didn't have her cake because she got sick and I forgot to take it out of the oven and it burned."

The congregation laughs. The laughter is calming and encourages me to go on.

"When Daddy said I should say something today, I got scared because I really didn't know what I should say. Why in the world I thought baking for you guys would be any easier is beyond me.

Mama always made me write about what I was thankful for — no matter how bad the situation. Sometimes I would get mad at her for making me find what she called the pineapple sugar in every situation. When she first told me she was sick, she even made me find the pineapple sugar in that.

Anyway, I have to be honest. Today, I never came up with anything to say that would help me or any of us find the pineapple sugar in Mama not being here with us anymore. But, still, I want to honor her in a special way. Just like Mama would want, I am searching for the pineapple sugar even in this situation. What I do have, even though Mama is gone, are the memories of sitting in the kitchen watching her make the pineapple sugar cake that we eat each year for Thanksgiving. It was always baked with love—the same love that is in the cake that you are about to get today, and today, so is mine. I hope that you all can taste the love inside of every bite. It may *not be perfect, but I think Mama would be proud. By the way, I made the cakes at home with a little help from my Daddy. I hope you'll enjoy."*

I look at Daddy, give him a smile, and nod to signal that it's time to pass out the cake. I then see him give the same nod to Reverend Bingham.

With a wave of Reverend Bingham's hand, the ushers begin handing out a slice of cake to everyone sitting in the church. Daddy and I had taken great care to cut the cakes into one-hundred individual slices to hand out during the service. As if they had handed out cake a thousand times during a church service, the ushers assume their posts and immediately jump into action. After just a few short minutes, everyone is holding their slice; the ushers take the leftover cake, forks and napkins to the table sitting at the back of the sanctuary.

I step to the microphone again.

"I would like each of you to take a few minutes as you enjoy your cake to think of Mama. Think about her smile, her laughter, her strength, and personality and everything else great about her. To help us do that, my Daddy is going to come up and sing a special song that he wrote for Mama a long time ago. We both thought it would be nice to share the song that she inspired with those who knew and loved her."

I hug Daddy as he walks up to the microphone. I whisper, "I love you, Daddy" as I move back to my seat where my slice of cake is waiting.

Without one spoken word, Daddy begins to play his guitar. As soon as I take the first bite of my cake, he starts with the first verse of *Josephine*. His song is almost like some kind of signal for the congregation, because as I look around, people actually begin to eat their cake.

Before I can worry about whether or not everyone likes the cake, I hear the music stop.

What's going on?

I look up from my cake slice just in time to see Daddy begin to cry as he lowers his head down toward his chest. His hands are still holding onto the guitar.

Seeing my father crumbling in front of everyone should make me feel helpless. But it doesn't. My Daddy is hurting and there is no way I am going to sit by and watch. I will not let him cry alone, especially not here and not now. In the back of my mind, I can almost hear Mama's voice say, *"Get up there, Safiri. Family is all we've got..."*

What I do next surprises even me. Without another thought, I step in front of the microphone, picking up where Daddy has stopped:

... There'll still be time for a walk in the park
when summer blossoms from spring,
* And I'll still find a way to hum when my*
voice ain't strong enough to sing...

I sing. I sing the song the way that Daddy always sang his heart out to Mama. I close my eyes and belt out the melody Daddy had written to his first love, Josephine.

The music starts to play behind me. Daddy's fingers strike every chord with perfect tenderness.

His voice comes in behind mine, and what started out as a solo turns into an unexpected duet. Even though we have never practiced together, Daddy and I sing in perfect harmony.

While we sing, everyone eats and savors our cake as if we were at the Thanksgiving table. Members of the congregation nod their heads and pat their feet as Daddy and I finish our song:

The bright side will sometimes fade away,

But since pineapple sugar was my first love.

As long as she's in my heart, trouble can't tear
me apart

'Cause I'll see whatever life sees fit to teach-

Since pineapple sugar is always within my
reach.

When we come to the end, I open my eyes. Folks begin to clap in a way that makes me feel like a celebrity. One by one, people begin to stand, until the entire church is on its feet for our standing ovation that goes on for at least five minutes. Daddy reaches out, hugs me, and simply whispers, "You're just like your Mama."

The ushers begin collecting the trash, and Reverend Bingham dismisses us all from service. When it is all over, I see smiles that had not been there when we entered the memorial service. So many people come up and thank us for giving them such a special way to remember Mama. I have to admit that I feel proud of myself, making my first pineapple sugar cake–twelve of them to be exact. I am more proud that the memorial service of someone as cheerful as Mama has made people smile. This moment, I would have to say, has got to be the greatest pineapple sugar moment ever.

 epilogue:

Tuesday, November 4th

Dear Journal,

This year has been challenging but I have learned so much about myself. I turned thirteen and am finally in the upper school at Bringhurst Preparatory Academy. It seems like I have been waiting forever to get to eighth grade. To be honest, the rest of last school year was a little rough. I had to do it without Mama. Even worse was that when I came back to school after Mama's funeral, people *really didn't know what to say to me. The first few days were tough because I felt like everyone was staring at me, like the mold on one of our science experiments. Passing by Mama's old classroom every day and not seeing her standing at the door greeting her students became a constant reminder that she was gone. That was even harder.*

Maisy, Eileen, and Kimberly and even Michele have been great friends through this all. I am so glad that the four of us are back together again! Every night before bed, I always get a text message from at least one of them to tell me good night. They've made a pact with each other to do whatever it takes to keep me from crying too much. Ever since the funeral, Michele has come over nearly every weekend to help me "reinvent myself," as she calls it. With the help of Aunt Annie-Lou, she and I have organized my entire closet! Michele has even taught me her secret to always looking fabulous. I think Mama would have gotten a kick out of seeing me so stylish.

It has been almost a year since Mama died and not a day goes by that I don't think of her. My family promised that we will continue to celebrate Thanksgiving the same way we al-

ways have — with family, friends, food, and of course, Mama's pineapple sugar cake. Everyone will do their share to get Thanksgiving dinner on the table. Of course, I've been put in charge of baking Mama's pineapple sugar cake because no one else knows how to put the ingredients together the way I do. I've decided to keep the recipe a secret, too. Only Daddy's eyes have ever seen Mama's precious recipe.

I will miss Mama and all of the times that we spent each year together in the kitchen right before Thanksgiving. But, I am going to keep doing it – I will look for the pineapple sugar in every moment of my life and write about it while I bake the cake. It's difficult, but Mama taught me that the cake only works the way it is supposed to when I write about my pineapple sugar while it's baking. One thing I have learned on my own is that Thanksgiving is so much better once you have been able to give thanks for everything, even the bad things.

Mama is always going to be with me; her spirit is just too strong to ever really die. I know I will always be able to hear her voice while I'm searching for the pineapple sugar in good and bad times. That's worth more than anything in this world.

Whenever something bad happens, I will try to find the pineapple sugar just like Mama would want me to. What I have learned is that Josephine Fields was teaching me more than just how to bake a cake. She took the time to teach me that things happen just as they should and it is up to us to find a way to celebrate the good, even when it is hard to see it. So, although it will be hard, I will keep working on finding the pineapple sugar in losing Mama, just like she would want. Every year, I will sit down and write about it. I will keep telling the story of my life from one Thanksgiving to the next, and one day, the answer will come. It may not happen anytime soon, but I won't stop. As long as I keep searching for pineapple sugar in my life, even though Mama isn't here with me, she will live as long as I do.

For that, I will always be thankful.

Until next year,

Safiri Josephine Fields

3 1901 05841 0335